BEAUTY IN HIDING

BEAUTY IN FLIGHT BOOK 2

ROBIN PATCHEN

JDO PUBLISHING

To Ray Patchen
Korean War veteran
Father-in-law extraordinaire
And inspiration for Harold "Red" Burns

CHAPTER ONE

O f course it was raining.

And not merely raining. Harper had been white-knuckling the steering wheel of her used VW Jetta through an absolute deluge since Rhode Island. Visibility had been practically nonexistent on the interstate. After she'd exited onto the state highway that brought her to Nutfield, thanks to the lack of street lights, visibility had been no farther than a few feet in front of her car.

The constant swish-swish of the wipers was the only sound as she stopped at a T in the road. The area was deserted. Maybe that was normal in a little town for a Monday night at eight-thirty. She had no idea. She'd never lived anywhere this far off the beaten path.

She consulted her phone to check the map, but her navigation software was trying—and failing—to figure out where she was. Shocking that a fifty-dollar pay-as-you-go phone from the convenience store didn't work properly.

Fortunately, she'd studied the map enough at the last stop that she sort of knew where she was going. Sort of.

She glanced at Red, the elderly man in her care. His eyes were wide with worry, and she didn't blame him. He'd had a very difficult few days. Both of them had, but they'd survived this long. She'd keep Red safe even if it killed her.

Which it very well might.

She turned left and picked up speed. The car hit a puddle that had looked manageable, but water splashed against the windshield, momentarily blinding her. The wheels slid, and she hit the brake.

"Be careful!" Red shouted.

By the time she got the car under control, her heart had wedged in her throat.

She pulled into the breakdown lane, stopped, and rested her head against her hands on the steering wheel. They were okay. She hadn't careened off the side of this dark road and landed in a ditch. They were almost there.

If she remembered correctly, the street they were looking for wasn't far. She glanced in the rearview, which revealed no headlights, and maneuvered back into the lane, driving slowly to peer at the street signs.

And there it was. Thank God. She turned onto a street barely wide enough for two cars. The house they wanted was supposed to be the first on the left, but there were no houses anywhere. She'd driven about two hundred yards and was about to give up when she saw a driveway.

Harper checked the address on her phone, peered through the downpour at the mailbox, and focused on the house beyond. She could barely make out the shape of it in the rain. It was completely dark.

"Where in the blazes are we now, girl?"

Harper stretched her face into what she hoped would look like a smile and turned to the old man in the passenger seat. "We're home."

Red peered through the pouring rain. "This isn't home. This isn't anywhere near home."

She patted his leg. "It will be, soon enough."

He harrumphed, a reaction that had become familiar to her in recent days. Thanks to the traffic, the rain that had battered them all day, and Red's frequent need for stops, what should've been a five-hour drive from the hotel in Newark had become eight. Every bone in her body ached with exhaustion. She couldn't imagine how he felt.

She maneuvered the car beside the mailbox, pulled it open, and snatched the keys, but not fast enough to keep the rain from soaking the arm of her sweatshirt. It'd been a long time since she'd lived anywhere safe enough to leave keys in a mailbox. Maybe it was a good sign the landlord left them there. Maybe those keys meant that coming here wasn't the stupidest, rashest thing she'd ever done.

Not that she'd had a lot of choices.

She backed into the driveway so Red would be closer to the front door.

Gramps. Gramps. She had to get used to calling him Gramps.

"Let me unlock the house, then I'll come back for you."

"Don't you leave me out here." His words were gruff, but they didn't conceal the fear beneath them. As if she'd ever do anything to harm him. As if she hadn't risked everything to protect him.

But he didn't know that. He didn't know what she'd discovered about his grandson, Derrick, and he didn't remember the bodies he'd discovered in the living room of his home.

"I'll be right back. I promise." After she snatched her raincoat from the backseat and slipped it on, she pulled the hood over her head, and pushed open the door. Cold rain splattered against her jeans as she hurried around the car and up the steps. The wind whipped, blowing the hood of her jacket against her face and making it hard to see while she tried to shove the key in the lock. Finally, she opened the door.

Inside, she lowered her hood and took in the space. There were hardwood floors that needed to be refinished and off-white walls that looked freshly painted. A sofa and a recliner were separated by a side table, and a narrow coffee table stretched in front of the sofa. The furniture seemed, if not new, then only gently used. A fireplace was tucked into the wall on her right. What she wouldn't give for a blaze in there right now. An old TV stand stood empty against the wall beside her.

She crossed the living area into the kitchen. Small and functional. The cabinets were worn but clean—on the outside anyway. She opened the refrigerator door. Clean, and cold inside, so the landlord had made good on his promise to turn it on. A small round kitchen table had four chairs surrounding it.

Harper headed down the hallway toward the bedrooms. Just like the landlord had said, each had a bed and dresser. No bedding, but she'd taken care of that. The only bathroom was just before the smaller bedroom.

This would work.

She stared at the bed in the smaller room, her room, and fantasized about falling into it for a nap. She and Gramps had been in New Jersey by the time the sun rose Friday morning. They'd spent the weekend in a hotel near Newark. On Friday, she'd treated Red for antifreeze poisoning after doing extensive research on what could have been slipped into his Gatorade based on his symptoms. Everything matched, and lucky for her, antifreeze could be flushed from the body with alcohol. Lucky for her, but not for Red. She'd given him multiple doses of his *medicine*—straight vodka—for twenty-four hours. Once the hangover faded, he seemed weaker than when she'd begun. His dementia had been worse than ever, though that might have been in part due to the unfamiliar surroundings. But the effects of the poison had worn off.

Maybe she'd saved him. The cure was awful, but alcohol wouldn't kill him. Antifreeze would.

Using Gramps's debit card, she'd taken the daily limit out of his checking account every day, done some shopping, and searched for a place to live. She figured Derrick would assume she'd headed southwest, since that's the direction she'd come from, so she'd searched northeast and found this place in rural New Hampshire. The price was right, the location so random, nobody would think to look for them here. Now that they were settled, she couldn't use the debit card again. Too easy to track.

Now, she was in a rental home in New Hampshire. Nobody would find her here. But could she discover what had happened back in Maryland? Until she did, she and Red would have to stay hidden. Gramps. She and *Gramps* would have to stay hidden.

She pulled her hood up again and rushed through the rain to the car, where she took Gramps's walker out of the trunk and unfolded it. Then she opened his door.

"Took you long enough." He was staring at the house, his voice raised to be heard over the rain. "What are we doing here?"

"This is our new home."

He crossed his arms. "I want to go back to my house. I don't like this one."

"I know," she said. "Let's just go inside and check it out. You've got to be tired of this car."

He stared at the house, then at her, then at the house again. Finally, he blew out an angry breath. "I'm not gonna like it."

"That's the spirit." She stood back, left the walker close by, and helped him turn so his feet were on the driveway. The events of the previous few days—the poison, the treatment, and seeing those dead men, not to mention running for their lives and staying in a shady hotel—had left him weaker than she'd ever seen him. "Come on out, Gramps."

"Why you keep calling me that?"

She'd explained it to him, but he'd forgotten her desire for people to believe they were related. Now wasn't the time to go over it again, so she ignored the question while he tried to stand. Couldn't seem to make it. She moved the walker out of his way. "Let me help."

"Don't need your help." But he gripped her forearms like he might a lifesaver in the ocean. She hid the pain his grip caused. The bruise on that arm wasn't his fault. He didn't even know it was there.

She eased him out, then steadied him on his feet and adjusted his fedora. At least his head would stay dry. He leaned on the door while she got his walker into position.

"Can you just—?"

"I got it," he snapped.

Shuffling, they made their way through the rain to the front porch steps. Just three. Should be no trouble, considering at home he navigated an entire flight of stairs every day.

She lifted the walker to the landing, positioned herself on one side while he gripped the wrought-iron handrail on the other. He got his grips right, but when he tried to step up, he couldn't quite make it and rocked back down.

"Let's try that—"

"I don't need your help."

But he didn't move.

He'd been sitting too long. After the poisoning and the antidote, his legs were too weak to make this work. And he was embarrassed.

She forced a deep breath, wiped rainwater out of her eyes, and said as brightly as she could, "Let's give it another shot."

He put his stronger leg on the step, rocked forward. She helped as much as she could and cursed the sprain in her wrist. If not for that, this would be easy. As it was, pain shot up her arm as she took his weight.

He made it to the first step.

Then stopped.

"Two more."

"I can count."

She waited for him to catch his breath. When the rain had thoroughly soaked through her sneakers, she said, "You ready?"

He lifted his foot, rocked forward, and tried. She could feel his effort. Tears filled her eyes from the ache in her arm. Normally, getting up three steps would be no problem. He strained, she strained, and they made it to the second step.

A car splashed by on the street behind them. She didn't turn to see. It wasn't as if it would be a friend. She didn't have any of those, not in this town. Not anywhere.

After a moment's rest, Gramps lifted his foot to the landing, took a deep breath, and rocked forward.

His hand slipped on the rail, and he fell forward. Instinct had her grabbing him. Pain shot up her arm, and gravity pulled him down. He banged his shoulder against the railing and barely got his hand down in time to keep himself from landing face-first on the concrete. He turned, sat on the step, and stared at the wooded front yard.

She sat beside him and buried her face in her hands. Hot tears joined the cold rain. Neither spoke.

What was she doing? How could she protect this man when she couldn't even get him into the house?

Father, help.

She'd begged God for help all weekend. Begged him to make Red better. And He had. Red had woken up today looking better than he had in a week. His bright eyes and the color in his face, the concern in his expression and the joy in his smile had been a blessing. This morning, feeling both grateful and helpless, Harper had decided to embrace the God Gramps and her friend Estelle trusted so completely. She'd been trying, trusting, failing, and trying again for months. That morning, her decision made, she'd felt able to conquer the world. There was a God, and He loved her.

She'd been sure of it.

Now, the world was dark and gray and closing in on her.

A real Christian would know how to pray. Harper didn't know anything about God except what Red and Estelle had told her and what little she'd understood from reading her Bible. If she was wrong about God, then she was lost.

Maybe she was lost anyway.

"Can I help?"

She looked up and wiped her eyes as a man jogged down the driveway. He wore a jacket, jeans, work boots, and a baseball cap. A pickup was parked on the road in front of the house. A total stranger. A man.

"Who are you?"

He stopped at the bottom of the steps and smiled up at them as if conversing in a storm were the most normal thing in the world. "Jack Rossi."

Jack Rossi. This was their new landlord? They'd only corresponded through email, but for some reason, she'd pictured a middle-aged, gray-haired man. She'd been very wrong.

"I presume you're Harper Cloud."

She wiped moisture from her eyes and attempted a smile. "We were just admiring the view."

The man's grin only got wider as he focused on Red... Gramps... who was watching him through narrowed eyes. "Let's do formal introductions inside, shall we?"

Gramps nodded once, turned, and reached for the railing to pull himself up. She started to position herself on his other side, but Jack stopped her with a touch on her shoulder. He said nothing, just lifted his eyebrows and nodded toward the old man. *May I?*

She wanted to cry all over again, though she wasn't sure why. Because she didn't want to need help? Because she did need it? Because somehow, God had actually answered her prayer?

She opened the door while Jack put Gramps's arm over his shoulder and helped him up. They maneuvered into the house in no time.

Thank God for Jack Rossi.

CHAPTER TWO

The old man's teeth were chattering, and he seemed too worn out to speak. Jack helped him shuffle through the living room and ease into the recliner.

The woman stood in the doorway dripping rainwater from her coat and a hood that obscured her face. Jack asked, "The rest of your stuff is in the car?"

"I can get it."

"There's a quilt in the closet in the master. Why don't you grab that?" He cut his gaze toward the old man.

She paused a moment, nodded to the keys she'd tossed on the coffee table, and headed down the hall.

Jack snagged the car keys, ducked through the rain, and popped her trunk. He lifted a large fancy suitcase, a smaller beat-up suitcase, and a giant department store sack. He returned to drop the things inside before running back out. Seemed the woman had loaded up on groceries. He hooked the bags over his arm and grabbed a case of Gatorade and took them to the kitchen. Back outside, he checked the trunk one more time before opening the rear door. A box containing a brand new flat-screen TV was positioned on the backseat. A purse and a small duffel bag were on the floor behind the passenger seat. He hooked the purse and duffel around his arm and then pulled out the TV. It was a decent size with a handle on the top of the box to make it easy to carry. He slammed the car door with his hip and hurried inside to keep the box from getting too wet.

In the living room, he set the TV box in front of the stand and the purse and duffel on the sofa.

Harper's back was to him as she helped the man out of his wet jacket. She was still wearing hers. Probably too chilled to take it off.

He should take his off, too. Not that he hadn't already dripped all over the living room and kitchen. And he hadn't exactly been invited to stay. "What can I do?"

"We got it," she said, not bothering to turn. "Thanks."

She got the old man's jacket off, set it beside the hat on the hearth, then tucked the quilt around him. "You warming up?"

"It's colder than a witch's—"

"Gramps..."

The man's words died as Harper backed away, shed her own jacket, and turned toward Jack. "Thanks for your help."

"Uh..." Whatever he'd been about to say died on his lips. Holy cow, she was beautiful. Straight blond, shoulder-length hair, blue eyes, Hollywood cheekbones. And a body that made him congratulate himself for noticing she had a face.

Her eyebrows lifted as if she knew what he was thinking.

"Right," he said. "No problem. Good thing I happened along when I did."

"We'd have made it." She crossed her arms and attempted a smile, though the effort looked painful. "We just needed a little rest."

He let the comment pass and turned to the man. "I'm Jack."

"I'm not deaf," he said. "Heard you outside." The gruff words were barely out before he broke into a smile. "Harold Burns. But everybody calls me Red, on account of my luxurious red hair." He ran a hand over his head, which was bare as a dog's belly.

Jack shook the man's hand. His fingers were ice. "Great to meet you, Mr. Burns."

"Didn't you hear me, boy? It's Red."

"Okay, Red." He turned to Harper, who was staring at the bags on the floor. She looked like she wanted to cry. He was pretty sure, based on the red in her eyes, that the moisture on her face when he'd found them was from more than rain. "Why don't I take those back to the bedrooms for you. Which ones go where?"

"I can do it," she said.

He swallowed his sarcastic answer. "I bet you've had a heckuva day. Let me help."

He was sure she was going to argue. Then, her shoulders slumped. "Yeah, okay. Thanks. The bigger suitcase goes in the bigger room, the smaller one and the duffel in my room."

He glanced at the smaller suitcase, which was fastened closed with duct tape. "Nice luggage." He'd meant the words to be teasing, but added "no offense" when her back stiffened.

"It broke."

"I see that." He grabbed the things before she could change her mind and order him out of his own house.

His house, except he'd rented it to them. He had no right to be there. So far his plan to make his way in real estate was working out swimmingly.

Despite Harper's defensiveness, Jack was glad he'd seen them when he'd driven by. He'd been keeping an eye out for his new tenants all day, so he hadn't been surprised at the car in the driveway. He *had* been surprised to see two figures struggling up the steps.

He set the bags where she'd directed and returned to the living room. Red was staring at the box on the floor. In the kitchen, Harper had opened cabinets and was staring inside. They were all clean, lined with fresh liner, and, of course, empty.

"You looking for something?" he asked.

She pulled a cell phone from her jeans' pocket, peered at it, and tossed it on the countertop. "Piece of crap."

"No service?"

"Can't even order a pizza. I guess it's cold sandwiches."

He cut his gaze to the shopping bags. Clearly, she was too tired to cook.

"I have a phone you can borrow," he said. "Better yet, why don't I run home and grab some dinner? I made a pot of chili tonight, and there's plenty to share. You guys like chili?"

"I don't—"

"We love chili," Red shouted.

She lowered her voice. "He loves it, but spicy food doesn't agree with him."

"Still not deaf," Red yelled.

She closed her eyes, dropped her head.

Jack had the sudden urge to laugh, which he was smart enough to stifle. "I have some chicken and gnocchi soup in the freezer. I can defrost it and be back in a flash."

She turned again to the empty cabinets, opened the empty drawers. "I don't know why I thought *furnished* meant there'd be dishes."

Ah. She had nothing to cook with or eat on.

"It's not a timeshare," he said.

"I know that. I just..."

When she didn't finish, he said, "Why don't you sit?"

She stared at the table, didn't move. "Been sitting for twelve hours."

"And you look like you're about to drop." He stepped out of the doorway and gestured to the sofa. "Have a seat. I'll take care of dinner, and after you've eaten, you can regroup. Okay?"

She seemed to be formulating an argument, so he walked away. There was another quilt still in the house, a castoff from the previous owners. He'd thought to take the handmade blankets home with him, maybe try to sell them like he planned to do with the rest of the stuff the previous owners had left. Most of that was still in his garage collecting dust. But the quilts were too nice to leave out there, and his house was always in some stage of reconstruction. He'd forgotten about them until tonight. He snatched the quilt from the closet in Harper's room intending to use it to entice her to sit, but when he returned, he found her half sitting, half lying across the sofa. He draped it over her, and she smiled.

Oh, man. That was the kind of smile that could compel a man to wrestle giants.

"Thanks," she said. "You're right. I'm so tired, I can't think."

"Been there."

She glanced past him to the TV box, and he debated. Entertainment or food? Maybe a little escape from reality would do them both good.

"Don't just stand there, boy," Red said. "Set it up. Let's see if there's anything on."

"Okey-doke. I'll see what I can find." He removed the packaging, got the TV out, and plugged it in. It went through its start-up sequence, finally finding a few channels. Not a lot, but without cable or satellite, it was all they'd get. "Looks like we have news, cartoons, or *Frasier* reruns."

"*Frasier*." Red left no room for arguing, and Harper didn't seem to care.

"I'll be back in a little bit." He focused on Harper. "For now, just rest. Okay?"

"I don't need..." But her argument was cut-off by a yawn.

"I'll take that as a yes." He walked out before she could stop him.

CHAPTER THREE

Derrick Burns had stayed home all weekend, certain with every noise and slamming door on the street outside his Baltimore condo that the police were coming to arrest him. There would be no evidence against him. After Harper had confronted him the other night, Derrick had snuck in the side door of the garage and retrieved the contaminated Gatorade bottles. Then, he'd taken them to a fast-food restaurant along I-95, dumped the contents into the bathroom sink, and rinsed the bottles before he'd stuffed them in the trash can. By now, those bottles were in a landfill somewhere.

The police wouldn't be able to prove a thing.

Assuming Harper had figured it out. He didn't think she had. There'd just been a bunch of open bottles. But he couldn't be too safe. Or maybe paranoia was closing in.

Derrick went to work on Monday as if everything were normal. He had a good day, made some money for his clients—and for himself. He landed a few new clients, too. It had been months since he'd lost Russell Caldworth's business—lost it thanks to Harper. Since then, Derrick had built his clientele up again, so now he had more clients and managed more accounts than ever.

Screw Russell. Screw Russell's rich friend, Constantine. Screw Harper. He didn't need them. He didn't need anybody.

He did need two hundred thousand dollars.

And fast.

The thought of the money he owed brought back the image of Harper's bruised cheek, the cut on her neck he'd seen Thursday night. At the time, he'd felt terrible, but the further he got from that day, the clearer he saw it. It was her fault he didn't have the money to get out of debt. If she'd supported him at the beach house last summer instead of working against him all weekend, he'd have kept Russell's business and landed Constantine's, too. If she'd just given in and let him stay with her, he wouldn't have lost that night's poker game to Carter. He'd had to pay the snake almost all that had remained in his checking account. A few thousand dollars, but he'd needed it to make a good-faith payment to Quentin.

Quentin Gray, the scariest moneylender in Vegas, was after Derrick. And it was Harper's fault.

And she was going to fix it.

After work that Monday, he drove straight to Gramps's house, pounding his steering wheel and directing more than a few curse words at the other drivers slowing him down. Morons, all of them.

He had two goals for this visit. To get back into Gramps's good graces—he should have done that months before—and to make up with Harper. He needed her on his side. He needed her to help him convince Gramps to loan him the money. And it would be a loan. Derrick could make it back, no problem. He'd get on a payment plan with Gramps. He just needed a few more clients, and he'd have the extra cash he needed to keep Gramps off his back. As if the old man needed it.

The rich cheapskate, gripping his money is his old, wrinkled fists.

Derrick had to get Gramps to loosen that grip, or Gramps's supposedly beloved grandson would be the next one with the bruises. And Quentin's goons wouldn't be as gentle with Derrick as they had been with Harper.

He rubbed his knee instinctively.

He'd heard of broken kneecaps, crushed feet. Nothing bad enough to keep a guy from working, but a lesson he'd never forget.

He parked in the circular drive in front of the house, glanced at his image in the rearview mirror, and practiced his humble smile.

He could do this. He had to do this.

When nobody came to the door at his knock, he used his key and let himself in. "Harper? Gramps?"

The house was silent. The TV wasn't even on.

He started in the kitchen. Empty. The living room was empty, too. He crossed to the back door and reached for the deadbolt, but it was already unlocked. Odd. Maybe they were out back, but a quick look proved the yard was empty.

He ran up the steps. Nobody in Gramps's room. He opened Harper's door, stepped into the sacred space.

Sacred because she'd never let him in.

As if she were so pure. He knew better.

Her room was empty, too. He was tempted to go inside, look around, touch her things, just because he could. Because she'd kept so much of herself from him.

Because she owed him.

But they'd probably just gone to get something for dinner. They'd be home any minute.

So he closed the door and went to the kitchen, where he poured himself a glass of ice water.

And he waited.

But an hour passed, and they still weren't home.

He dialed her phone number. It went straight to voice mail. "I'm at the house," Derrick said. "I wanted to check on Gramps, see how he was feeling. Where are you guys?"

He figured he'd get a call back, but ten minutes passed, fifteen. Weird.

He checked the fridge, but there was nothing worth eating in there. He'd check the garage freezer, maybe find a frozen meal he could heat up. He opened the door and froze.

The Caddy was gone—he'd expected that.

But Harper's car was gone, too.

That made no sense at all. Gramps didn't drive anymore. How could both cars be gone?

Where were they?

He forgot about eating and returned to the kitchen and dialed her phone again.

Voice mail again.

Something wasn't right.

He sat, skimmed through his phone, and checked his email. Got one from his bank and clicked on it, but the link seemed broken. Everything was messed up today. Didn't matter. He knew what his bank was going to tell him. He was out of cash.

And without Harper and Red, he was out of luck.

CHAPTER FOUR

Harper forced her eyes open. Thanks to her wet jeans and socks, her legs were freezing.

She heard a man's voice, a low chuckle, and clanging dishes.

The TV was on but muted.

Red's chair was empty.

She sat up, fought a wave of pain and dizziness, and stood. "Gramps?"

"Don't get your knickers in a knot," he called. "I'm fine."

His voice came from the direction of the kitchen behind her, so she stepped that way and froze.

Red...Gramps...was seated at the kitchen table sipping from a steaming mug.

Jack smiled over his shoulder as he stirred a steaming pot of something that smelled of chicken and some heavenly spice she couldn't identify. "Have a nice nap?"

"How'd you get in?" That was a stupid question, though. Had she even locked the door?

One eyebrow lifted. "You always wake up so cheerful?"

She tried to come up with a good retort but was silenced by a shudder. She should've changed out of her wet clothes before she'd fallen asleep. She crossed her arms and eyed the steamy mug in Gramps's hand.

"Go change into something warm and cozy," Jack said. "I'll have a cup of tea waiting when you get back."

She stared at him. This man, this total stranger, was going to make her tea?

She squinted at him. What was his angle? Why was he there acting like a neighbor, a friend? She nodded toward the mug Gramps held. "That better be caffeine-free, or he'll be up all night."

Jack's smile stayed in place, maybe even got a little wider as if he found her amusing.

His response made her want to growl at him, but he'd probably break into raucous laughter.

Jack tapped the side of his head with his fingertips. "Actually thought of that." He looked at Gramps and added, "When you got a face as pretty as this"—he circled an invisible outline of his face with his free hand—"they think you must have all the brains of a sweet potato."

Gramps lifted his cup in a sort of salute. "Happens to me all the time, son. All the time."

The men chuckled at their brilliance.

She maybe did growl a little as she turned toward her bedroom. Just what she needed, some man to give Gramps more material.

When she reached her room, she froze. Her bed was made with the cheap bedding she'd bought on sale. The suitcase had been left on the bed.

Gramps couldn't have maneuvered around it with his bad hips and back. And he'd been too tired to do anything.

Which meant Jack, a total stranger, had found her sheets and stretched them across the bed. He'd pulled the comforter on, made sure it draped evenly over both sides. He'd stuffed her pillowcase with the pillow on which she'd lay her head.

Even as she marveled at the kindness, the image of his hands on her bedding made her shudder again.

She tore the duct tape from her luggage and dug through it looking for something warm.

A total stranger had come into her house, had made her bed, and was now fixing her tea. And her dinner. What kind of weird dimension had she and Gramps landed in? Because nothing in her experience had ever led her to believe that men like Jack existed outside of romance novels. He might have been joking about the pretty face, but he hadn't been wrong. The man was good-looking in a rugged, flannel-shirt-and-work-boots kind of way. Though he may have looked different from the men in her past, she'd learned the hard way that no matter what a man wore—suits and ties, joggers and sweatshirts, or jeans and flannel—men were not to be trusted.

She found a clean pair of jeans and a sweatshirt. Then she pulled something else out of the bag. Her fleece pajamas. Baggy, fluffy, ugly, pink fleece pajamas.

He'd said to slip into something warm and cozy. These fit the bill.

She peeled off her still-wet clothes, careful with her wrist, which was more tender after the debacle on the porch steps, and climbed into the fuzzy warmth. With a cup of something hot, she just might warm up before spring.

She touched the cut on her neck. It was healing. Hopefully, Jack wouldn't notice it.

What did he want from her? If he was like every other man she'd ever known, at least every one who wasn't so old he needed a little blue pill and an hour's notice, she could guess exactly what he wanted.

She pulled on a pair of dry socks and slipped her feet into her furry slippers.

Nothing said no-way-not-gonna-happen like furry yellow slippers.

She shuffled back to the kitchen and leaned against the doorframe. Now that the sleepy haze had worn off, she noticed all the changes since she'd first seen the room. Stuff...everywhere.

"I hope you don't mind." Jack adjusted the heat on the stove and turned to face her. He started to say something, stopped, and said, "Nice jammies."

"They're warm."

Their eyes met and held for a second before he cleared his throat and turned back to the stove. If she wasn't mistaken, a flush of pink climbed up his neck as he poured water from a saucepan into another mug, added a tea bag, and handed it to her.

"Thank you." She heated her hands on the warm cup and inhaled the scent. Smelled like cinnamon and something heavenly she didn't recognize. "This is perfect."

"Some kind of herbal something," Jack said. "I thought it would warm you up and help you relax." He stirred the soup. "When I bought this house, it was filled with... Well, it seemed like junk. All that stuff was still in my garage, and I remembered..." He turned to the counter, pointed at an old microwave and a toaster. Behind the toaster...was that a coffee maker? "No idea if they work."

She eyed the appliances, thought of what they represented. Coffee and food. Glorious—and easy—food. Her eyes tingled. Seriously, what was wrong with her? "That's... Thank you so much."

"We cleaned them up," Jack said. "The microwave was...well, it's clean now."

Gramps added, "It looked like someone had nuked a rat in there."

"Nice visual." She couldn't help smiling.

"Smelled like it, too," Gramps added. "But we got it clean."

"You helped?"

"Not like you were gonna do it," the old man said, "snoring and drooling on the sofa out there."

"I was not!"

She glared at Gramps, whose eyes crinkled with his smile. Proud of himself, the old codger.

Jack opened the cabinet, though not before she saw the corners of his lips twitch in an almost grin.

She was stifling her amusement when she caught sight of what was in the cabinet. Plates, bowls, cups.

"What did you...? Where did all that stuff come from?"

"Oh," Jack said. "I had some extras. Didn't have much silverware, but I grabbed a box of plastic ware at the store. Should hold you over 'til you go shopping. There's a little convenience store in Nutfield for essentials, but you'd be better off starting at the Walmart in Epping. Cheaper than our local store."

Cheap was good. Cheap was necessary.

She spied a sack on the floor beside Gramps. Snatching it up, she asked, "How long was I asleep?"

"Couple hours, if you drifted right off," Jack said.

"Hours? I can't have!" That would mean it was nearly nine o'clock. She sat at the table and looked around for a clock, but there was none. Her phone...she'd tossed it somewhere earlier.

"Girl, you haven't slept in days," Gramps said. "I'm just glad you got us here without snoozing at the wheel and killing us both."

"I would never..." She glanced at Jack, who'd gone back to stirring the concoction on the stove. "I was wide awake when I was driving. Just... I guess..."

Jack grabbed bowls from the cabinet. "Tired, obviously."

"She works too hard," Gramps said.

"Works?" Jack ladled some soup into a bowl, shooting her a glance over his shoulder. "All I've seen her do is sleep."

"Trust me, son. She works like a dog. Doesn't get enough rest."

She cleared her throat. "I'd prefer you didn't talk about me as if I weren't in the room."

"Well, go on, then. Get out." Gramps waved his hand toward the hallway, then laughed at his joke. "It sure was easier when you were sleeping."

She ignored the remark and looked in the grocery sack. She found a box of plastic forks, spoons, and knives.

Jack slid a bowl of soup in front of her. "Red had only nice things to say about you."

There was that kindness again. What was she supposed to do with that?

But what had Red...Gramps said? The man was more lucid tonight than he normally was at this hour, amazing considering the day they'd had. It figured that the one night she needed his dementia to flare up, he'd be clear-thinking.

Had he exposed her? She glanced at the old man, who winked at her. When she turned toward Jack, he was setting another bowl of soup on the table, and he seemed content, guileless, and utterly without suspicion. How long could that last?

She opened the package of plastic ware and handed a spoon to Gramps.

He grunted his thanks.

Jack slid into the chair beside them.

"No soup?" she asked.

"I ate chili earlier. Go ahead."

She lifted her spoon, then set it down when she caught Gramps's pointed look. Apparently, even though Jack was there, even though this was the most surreal experience in the world, Gramps would still pray.

He set both of his old, wrinkled hands on the table. She took one. After a moment's pause, Jack took his other. Gramps eyed them both until she and Jack closed the circle with their joined hands.

While Gramps prayed, she tried not to think about the warmth and strength of Jack's grip.

Men often seemed that way at first, didn't they? But they always had a reason behind their kindness.

Considering all Jack had done for them already, she had little doubt about what he was after.

CHAPTER FIVE

Derrick's phone alarm woke him at five a.m. It took him a minute to remember... He'd spent the night at Gramps's house. He figured he'd hear them when they got home from wherever they'd been, and he'd left his door open to be sure.

But nothing had awakened him all night long.

He pulled on the pants he'd worn the day before and walked down the hallway. Gramps's door was open, and the bed was empty. He looked in Harper's room and found the same thing.

They hadn't come home, and they hadn't called.

Where were they? Where would she go?

He would stay to confront her when she got back, but he had to work. So he left a note on the kitchen table—*Where are you guys? I'm worried. Please call as soon as you see this.* And he left for the long drive back to Baltimore. He'd be lucky to get home and showered and to work on time.

Another thing he could blame on Harper Cloud.

Despite her pretty face and gorgeous body, she was more trouble than she was worth. After all he'd done for her, she'd betrayed him again and again.

Because if Gramps were in the hospital, Harper would have

called. If he were sick, she would have called. She hadn't called, and she wasn't home.

When he found her, she'd be sorry she ever crossed him.

25

CHAPTER SIX

The deluge that began on Saturday continued into this Tuesday morning. The leaves had changed and fallen weeks before, and the snow wouldn't start for another month. The tourists stayed home in November, giving Jack more time than usual to work on his real estate business.

The house he lived in and the one next door had come as a package deal, a great deal, but they both needed a lot of work. He'd decided to live in this one while he fixed it up and rent the other to offset some of the costs.

Which was how he'd come to meet Harper and Red.

How had their night gone? With no phone, they had to feel cut off from civilization. He'd tried to help, which had earned gratitude from Red and suspicion from Harper.

In his experience, people who didn't trust others often couldn't be trusted themselves. What was Harper hiding behind that pretty face?

So much of what he'd seen the night before had felt incongruous. The old man's suitcase was high-dollar, but hers had been falling apart. Her jeans had looked several steps above what a person could find on a Target clearance rack, not that he was any kind of expert on fashion. Even soaking wet, they'd sure looked good on her. The Volkswagen was beat up, but both Red's jacket and hers were good brands. He might not know jeans, but he knew L.L. Bean.

And then there was the address she'd put on the rental application. Call him paranoid, but renting to someone he'd never met before had made him nervous, especially when it all happened in a matter of days. He'd put the house up for rent on Friday, she'd contacted him on Saturday, and they'd arrived on Monday. Who relocates to another state that fast? Of course he'd done a credit check. Harper Cloud didn't have much in the way of credit history, but there was nothing that struck him as unusual.

He'd also checked out her current residence. The address she listed was located in Maryland and worth over a million dollars. The property in Maryland was owned by Harold Burns. Red.

Why were they living in a dumpy rental when he owned a million-dollar home?

Incongruous.

Jack finished sanding the baseboards and stood to admire his work. Dust hovered in the air and landed on his plastic-covered furniture and TV, which he'd pushed to the middle of the room before starting the project. After he painted the baseboards in the entire house, he'd refinish the hardwood floors until they gleamed. He'd already replaced all the windows and painted all the walls. Next, he'd tackle the bathrooms and the kitchen.

He stared out the new bay window at the front yard. The rain was tapering off, the sun trying to peek through the thick clouds and trees that surrounded his property. As usual, the street out front was quiet. There were only a handful of houses on this narrow side road.

He showered, dressed, and debated what to do. Because he couldn't stop thinking about his new neighbors. Finally, he walked the hundred yards or so between their houses before he could talk himself out of it.

The Jetta was in the same spot where she'd parked it the night before.

At the front porch, he stopped. Of course they hadn't left. Red couldn't navigate the steps.

Jack quickly calculated the cost of adding a ramp and groaned. He had to do it, little though he wanted to.

He made it to the front door and was about to knock when he heard a crash inside.

Then a roar of anger. "Why are you doing this to me?" Red screamed.

"Gramps, stop—"

"Stop calling me that." His voice rumbled and shook. "I don't know you."

Jack knocked on the door. "Everything okay?"

Harper said, "Now's not a good—"

"Help!" Red's shout sounded terrified. "Help me!"

Jack tried the knob, but the door was locked. "Harper, open the door."

"Help!" The man's cries continued. "Help, help, help! She's gonna kill me. Help!"

Jack pounded on the door. "Open up, or I'll break it down."

He barely heard Harper over the old man's screams. "I'm coming. Hold—"

Another crash sounded through the door.

Jack yanked his keys from his pocket and fished for the right one.

The door opened.

Harper stood on the other side, tears streaming down her cheeks, an angry gash on her forehead near her hairline. A small drop of blood was making its way into her eyebrow. Before he had time to react, she turned and crossed to Red, who was standing in front of the recliner.

"Help me!" He looked like a different person from the one Jack had met the night before. His skin was mottled and red, his eyes were wild. His hands were fisted, trembling.

"Gramps, sit down." Harper stood in front of him, reached for his arms, but he slapped her hands away.

"Get away from me!"

"Please. I know it's—"

"Don't touch me!" Red looked past her at Jack. "You've got to help me. She kidnapped me!"

Jack focused on Harper again. "What happened?"

"He didn't sleep well, and he doesn't remember—"

"She's a liar, a liar. I have no idea who that woman is. You have to get me out of here."

"Okay, okay." Jack didn't know what else to say as he crossed the room. He glanced at Harper. "Why don't you go in the other room?"

"You don't know how to handle him."

Gramps screamed. "I want to go home! Somebody take me home!"

"All right." Jack ignored Harper and focused on Red. "You need to sit down and tell me about your home, okay? Can you do that?"

"I have to go." But the old man seemed to be losing steam.

"You will," Jack said. "Soon. But first, I need to get my truck. And I need to know where we're going. Just…" He gently took the man's upper arms in his hands. "Let's just sit and make a plan, okay?"

He could feel Harper behind him but didn't chance a glance. He'd heard of this, dementia patients getting angry and aggressive. He'd never witnessed it and had no idea how to handle it. By the looks of things, Harper hadn't done such a bang-up job on her own.

Red settled into the chair with a harrumph. "Take me home."

"Where is your home, Red?"

The man blinked at the use of his name. "Do I know you?"

"I'm Jack. We met last night."

The man seemed to accept that without question. "My house is in Maryland. Maryland."

"I bet it's nice."

"Yes. In Maryland. This isn't Maryland." The man nodded, his lower lip trembling. The fight was gone. Red's voice was high-pitched, nearly a sob. "I want to go home."

"I know."

Behind Jack, the TV came on. A game show, by the sound of it. The volume went up, and Red focused on the screen.

Jack sat back on his heels and turned to see Harper. She settled on the arm of the couch and watched Red. They stayed like that for a few minutes—her watching Red, Jack watching them both. He didn't know if the tirade was over or if Red would start again. Tears streamed down Harper's cheeks. The wound on her forehead was dripping, and she dabbed at it with the sleeve of her sweatshirt.

Red seemed to have forgotten the whole incident.

Jack stood and faced Harper. "Can we talk in the kitchen, please?"

Her gaze flicked to Red, to the TV, to him. She stepped into the adjacent room, where she settled into a chair, propped her elbows on the table, and dropped her face into her hands.

"What happened?"

She sighed, didn't look up. "He's done this before. Never that bad, though."

"He's under a doctor's care?"

Her head jerked up. Her glare was filled with malice. Or was that defensiveness? "Of course he is."

Jack started to speak, stopped at the sight of the blood dripping into her eyebrow. He scanned the counter, found the roll of paper towels he'd left the day before, and snagged one. He moistened it in the sink and kneeled in front of her chair. "That looks like it hurts."

She touched the cut with her ring finger and winced. "He didn't mean to do it."

Jack dabbed at the cut with the paper towel. It was bleeding badly. He pressed the towel against it, assessed her face for other wounds.

She met his gaze and leaned away. "I can hold it."

Their fingers touched as she took the paper towel, and she flinched.

Okay, then.

He rocked back on his heels, stood, and peeked into the other room. Red was focused on the game show, eyes vacant.

He turned back to Harper. "Why are you here?"

"We live here." Her voice was tired, as if she'd fought a war's worth of battles since he'd seen her last. "I have the paperwork to prove it."

"That's not what I mean."

"Why are *you* here?"

"I came to see if you needed anything."

"We're fine."

"Right. You had it well in hand when I arrived."

He waited for biting words, but her shoulders slumped. Her voice was barely a whisper when she said, "You have no idea."

When she said nothing else, Jack returned to the living room. Red was staring at the game show. Pieces of a broken coffee cup were scattered against the hearth beside his chair. Jack picked them up, saw blood on the jagged edge of what had been the cup's handle.

In the kitchen, he grabbed one of the plastic bags he'd brought in the night before and a couple of paper towels. He collected the broken shards of the cup, then wiped up the little bit of coffee that had spilled. Good thing the cup hadn't been full of hot coffee.

Once he had the mess cleaned, he returned to the kitchen and shoved the smaller plastic bag into the trash bag that lay crumpled on the floor beside the counter. He made a mental note to bring them a can—he was sure there was an extra in his garage—and sat at the table across from her. He kept his voice low and tried for kind. "I'm guessing he smashed the cup against the fireplace, then swung at you with the handle still in his hand."

"He wasn't trying to hurt me."

"I'm not judging. Just trying to understand."

She met his gaze, her eyes narrowed, her lips closed tight.

"That bruise on your arm. Did he—?"

"No!" She yanked down the sleeve of her sweatshirt, then the other one. She'd been careful to keep it covered the night before. He'd glimpsed it when she'd been sleeping. "Gramps didn't... I just... It's not important."

He studied her face. Was there a trace of a bruise on her cheek, too?

She turned away. "Gramps would never hurt me." She lifted the paper towel, looked at the red stain, and returned it to the wound. "It was an accident."

"The other bruises—"

"How is it any of your business?"

Good question. It didn't take him long to find a good answer. "Neighbors have to look out for each other. It seems you two could use a friend."

Her eyes widened, filled, and she dropped her face into her hand.

What was going on with these two? Where had her bruises come from? If that sweet old man was hurting her, what could Jack do about that?

How was he supposed to navigate this minefield?

And why couldn't he just leave them alone?

CHAPTER SEVEN

Why wouldn't Jack leave them alone? He was likable, handsome. Surely he had better things to do on a Tuesday than hang around her house. What was he after? Harper couldn't get the question out of her mind as she drove home from the store that afternoon. She was grateful that Jack had offered to hang out with Gramps so she could shop without dragging him along. Considering how tired Gramps was, Harper was happy to leave him at the house. The question remained, though—why was Jack Rossi being so nice to them?

She'd have to find a way to repay his kindness before he came up with his own plan.

The problem was, she had nothing to offer. Hardly any skills, barely enough cash to get by—and less of that after the trip to Walmart. No job, no prospects, no plans. She had no friends, no influence, no talent. She couldn't even afford to pick up a pizza to share for lunch.

She hated owing people.

One rash decision and her whole life was a big tangle of sticky threads she'd never straighten out. And that was okay. She'd known that going in, known she'd never be able to undo this decision, and she'd likely never recover from it. She could live with that after all

Gramps had done for her. But the memory of their terrible morning, Gramps's fear, then anger, then aggression. The dementia had never been this bad before. Sure, he'd been forgetful at times. When Derrick quit coming around, Gramps had fallen into a funk, which kept him from doing the activities he enjoyed—gardening, walks. He hadn't even been attending church as regularly. And now, Harper had ripped him away from everything he knew, everything familiar. Away from the home where he'd spent most of his life, from the memories, from the photographs and souvenirs of a life well lived.

Had there been another choice? She went over the facts again and couldn't see one. Anyway, what was done was done.

If only she'd remembered to bring that picture of Gramps's wife he always had with him. Of all the things to forget, she had to forget the one thing they couldn't replace.

She pulled up to the house. The night before, in the pouring rain, it had seemed creepy, but today the word *charming* came to mind. Sure, it needed a paint job and a lot of work on the inside, but nestled beneath the towering trees, the blue sky beyond the bare branches, the house seemed cozy and safe.

Please, let it be safe.

As she opened the car door, Jack stepped out of the house. "Can I help?"

"Sure."

She popped the trunk and grabbed a couple of the lighter sacks. Her wrist felt better, but she was careful with it. She needed it to be back to normal as soon as possible.

Jack somehow managed to wrangle the rest into his arms and slammed the trunk. "After you."

They dumped her purchases on the kitchen table. She peeked in the living room and checked on Gramps, who was sound asleep in the chair.

"He fell asleep half an hour ago," Jack said.

"He's had a rough couple of days."

Jack leaned against the door jamb.

She tried to ignore him as she put away her purchases—cheap plates, silverware, pots and pans and bowls. If only she could use Gramps's debit card. There was plenty of money in his account. But that would lead Derrick—and the police and whoever else was looking—right to her.

And then she'd miscalculated what was in her own account. She'd had to refuse some of the items, going through the sacks and pulling out things they could live without while the checkout girl and a guy in line behind her watched, sharing looks and checking their watches. Her face burned with shame and fear at the memory. She hadn't planned well enough. She and Gramps barely had enough food to last a week. She had a little cash left, and that wouldn't last long. And then what would she do?

She thought about the small package of turkey in the refrigerator. She had to offer to feed Jack. It was well past lunchtime, and Jack had fed them dinner the night before. She sent up a quick prayer, thinking of the Bible story about loaves and fishes. "Can I make you a sandwich?"

He flashed a smile, but his eyes didn't seem on board with his mouth. "I had a big breakfast."

"Okay." She turned away so he wouldn't see her relief. "I appreciate your help. You don't have to stay. I've got it from here."

When she got no response, she glanced at him. He hadn't moved except to cross his arms.

"What?"

"Did you get a job in Nutfield?"

"I need to find one." Soon. She opened the package of flatware and tossed the items in the sink to wash. A glance at Jack showed his eyes had narrowed to accusing slits. Or maybe she was only seeing a reflection of her own opinion, because she was a fool. An idiot and a fool who was in way too deep.

"So if you didn't move here for a job," Jack said, "why did you?"

"It's a very long story."

"Have you been here before?"

The container of oatmeal blurred as she remembered all those summers when she was a child. The cabin, the boat, the lake. The joy she'd always experienced. "My family used to vacation in a town like this."

"This is a vacation community. Not a lot of jobs this time of year."

She hadn't thought of that. She hadn't thought of much except *run, run, run.*

She tossed more silverware in the sink, the sound clanking and loud, and forced a bright smile. "I'll find something."

"What kind of work are you looking for?"

"Anything right now. Just—"

"And what will Red do while you're at work?"

If only she could hide until Jack went away. Because he was asking all the right questions, and she had no answers.

Run, run, run.

That was all she knew.

Her smile felt as fragile as thin glass. "It'll be fine. We'll figure it out. We have enough to get by."

He didn't speak, and she couldn't hold eye contact. She finished with the flatware, gathered the empty plastic bags, shoved them all in one, and stowed the bundle beneath the kitchen sink.

"Look," Jack said. "I have no idea what's going on with you or why you're here, but—"

"You don't have to worry about Gramps and me. We'll be fine. I've got it all worked out."

His eyebrows lifted, and he rocked back a shade before he recovered. "Right. Well, I'm sure that's true. There's a great little food pantry—"

"We don't need—"

"If you'd let me finish."

She tossed out a *go-ahead* wave, all the while thinking, *food pantry.* A food pantry. As much as she'd been about to argue with Jack, because, hey, the guy didn't need to know his renters were destitute, the words *food pantry* felt like a lifeline. Maybe they wouldn't starve this month.

Maybe.

"It's only open one day a week to customers, but they've just built a room on where a lot of older folks hang out. It's a recreation center for old people, and it's open Monday through Friday. They help with the pantry when they can. They like to be involved, but most of the time, they just watch TV, play cards, and talk. I was going to suggest that you see if Red likes hanging out with them. Maybe that'd be an option for when you're working."

"That sounds..." But words failed her, because, maybe, here was a solution. Maybe, here was a way out of the hole she'd dug for herself.

"Anyway," Jack said, "the pantry's open tomorrow at ten, if you want to go. You'll want to talk to the lady who runs it, Vanessa Baker. In fact, she might be able to hook you up with a job, too."

"Oh." Harper turned away, this time to hide the tears that seemed so close to the surface these days. She swallowed, sniffed, tried to rein in the emotions. Waited for Jack to say something.

When he didn't, she peeked back toward the door, but he wasn't there.

She wiped her eyes and saw Jack beside the couch watching the soap opera Gramps was missing thanks to his nap.

She took a deep breath and stood beside him. "You've been very kind to us. Thank you."

He turned to her, lowered his chin. "Happy to help." He headed for the door. "I'm going to get some supplies. I'll start building a ramp this afternoon. God willing, I'll have it finished by the time you guys need to leave tomorrow."

"You don't have to do that."

Jack raised his eyebrows and nodded toward Gramps.

"He can handle stairs," she said. "He was just tired."

Gramps's gruff voice cut off whatever Jack had been about to say. "Don't you guys talk about me as if I'm not in the room."

Harper turned and smiled at the old man. "I was just telling him how good you usually are on stairs. Right?"

His bushy gray eyebrows lowered over his tired eyes. "Most of the time."

Jack's smirk told her what he thought of that answer. "'Most of the time' doesn't cut it." Harper started to speak, but he cut her off. "And I don't want to hear how I don't have to, okay? I'm not having one of my tenants fall and break a bone because I was too cheap or lazy to offer a solution."

"But, it's—"

"I'll be back and forth, so if you see me outside, just ignore me. I'll have to take some measurements."

He was gone before she could argue.

CHAPTER EIGHT

It had been an exhausting day by the time Jack stepped into his house that night. Exhausting, but productive. It had taken until sundown, but he'd completed the ramp so Red could get in and out of the house without risk.

Now all he wanted to do was heat up some leftover chili and collapse into bed.

But the ramp wasn't all his new neighbors needed.

Not that any of it was his business, as he kept reminding himself. Harper and Red had issues, but they'd had issues long before he happened along. They'd brought those issues with them to Nutfield, and it was not Jack's job to fix them.

He shouldn't get involved. He had plenty to keep him busy, and he didn't need additional drama in his life. If he wanted to get his real estate business up and running this winter, he needed to stay focused.

But no matter how many times he told himself that, no matter how many times he berated himself for worrying about them, he couldn't get his neighbors off his mind.

So, fine. He'd do what he could. Then maybe he'd be able to drag his focus back to his own problems.

He grabbed his keys and headed to the food bank in town. He

knocked on the back door. A moment later, Vanessa Baker pulled it open.

"I figured you'd still be here," he said.

Behind the woman, a little girl yelled, "Who is it, Mommy?"

Vanessa opened the door wider and stepped into the storage area. "Come on in." Even with those three words, her accent was discernible. She spoke English well, but no one would mistake her for a native. Where she was from, Jack had no idea. Vanessa wasn't one to talk about her past and didn't seem open to questions.

As reticent as Vanessa was, her daughter was an open book—probably a fairy tale featuring wood nymphs and magic spells. The little girl had certainly cast a spell on him.

"Jack, Jack, Jack." Five-year-old Katarina barreled into him and wrapped her arms around his legs.

He lifted his hand to high-five her, feeling her mother's watchful eyes as he did. Had this been one of his nieces, he'd have lifted her up and hugged her, but Vanessa had rules about her daughter. No man was allowed to hug the girl. Even the old men who hung out in the rec center had to be careful.

More than once Jack had wondered what lay in Vanessa's past that caused her to be so cautious. Right now, he had another woman's problems to deal with.

He focused on the girl. "And how are you this fine evening, little kitten."

"I'm not a kitten." The girl's smile told him she liked his game.

"You're Kat, and little cats are kittens, right?"

She giggled. "I wanna show you something." And with that, she bolted through the doorway into the rec center.

He looked around the warehouse. It looked well-stocked for the clients who'd come the following day. In the morning, more groceries would be delivered, perishables picked up from nearby grocery stores. He didn't know how all that worked, but he'd been here often enough to marvel at the operation when the pickup trucks came in.

"You need something?" Vanessa asked.

"A favor."

She shifted to her back foot, narrowed her eyes.

Another defensive woman, as if he hadn't dealt with enough of that the last couple of days. "My new tenants," he said. "The old man looks like he needs some looking after, and his granddaughter needs to get a job. I wondered if it would be okay if the man hung out here."

"You know our policy. If he can't volunteer, then she has to if she wants to bring him."

"What if I volunteer in her stead?"

Vanessa flashed a rare smile. "You already volunteer many hours. Without your work, there wouldn't be a rec center."

He started to answer but stopped when Kat ran back into the room. "Look, look!" She waved a piece of paper up toward him.

He took it and gazed at the drawing. A cat and a kitten. He met Vanessa's eyes and lifted his brows before focusing on the girl. "You didn't draw this all by yourself, did you?"

"Mommy got me a book to teach me how to draw animals, and I copied it."

"Wow. This is really good. And all the fur, you did that, too?"

"Uh-huh. And the eyes. They were the hardest. In the book, I was just supposed to color them all in one color, but cats' eyes are pretty, so I wanted to make them look like real eyes."

They weren't perfect, but they had slit pupils and a little variation in the color. "You did a great job." He handed the paper back to the little girl and focused on Vanessa. "She's very talented."

"Yes." Vanessa looked at her daughter with affection before focusing on him again. "You think your tenant needs our services, food, anything else?"

"She claimed they were fine, but..." He thought of the sparse groceries, the state of her car, and the few items they'd brought with them. "If you tell her she has to be a client to leave Red here, then she'll be *forced* to get some groceries, which I think she needs."

Vanessa studied him, eyes narrowed and lips pursed, before

she nodded once. "Da. Yes, bring her tomorrow, and we will work it out."

"Thank you. Her name is Harper Cloud." He turned to Kat. "And thank you for showing me your beautiful picture. You're a very talented young lady."

"I'm only five."

He chuckled. "You sure? You seem so much more mature than that."

"I am." She looked at her mother. "Right, Mommy?"

"Yes, *ceri*."

Jack focused on the little girl. "What is '*ceri*'?"

Vanessa answered. "It means daughter in Serbian."

"Is that where you're from?"

"Da." She grabbed the doorknob. "You need anything else?"

Jack took the hint. "Nope. Thanks so much for your help. I'll send them over tomorrow. I'll be here, too, to install the crown molding."

Vanessa nodded. "Thank you. I will help your new tenants if I can."

———

CHAPTER NINE

Harper parked in the lot at the address Jack had given her. The food bank was a block off Crystal Avenue, Nutfield's main drag, and located in a small warehouse-type building. Though the tan metal sides weren't attractive, the area around the glass doors had been landscaped with evergreen shrubs so that even in November it looked inviting. Other vehicles were parked in the small lot, many clunkers like hers. Beyond a chain-link fence, she saw newer, fancier cars, pickups, and SUVs. Maybe that was where the workers parked.

"What are we doing here?" Gramps asked.

She couldn't very well tell him she was looking for elderly day care. "I'm going to see somebody about a job."

"You got a job. Taking care of me is your job."

"A little extra money never hurt."

"Let me call Roger and have him wire us some cash. You don't need to be working."

If only. But Roger Canfield, Gramps's attorney, would demand to know where they were and why they'd left. Could he be trusted? Were the police looking for her? The thought left her hands trembling as she stared at the doors. She couldn't go in there. They'd ask for ID, and what would happen then? Would her name be put in some online system? Would it trigger an alert? Would the local cops realize they had a fugitive, an ex-con, in their sleepy little town?

They'd call Derrick. Derrick, who'd been poisoning his own grandfather.

She couldn't risk it.

She'd reached for the gear shift to reverse out of the spot when a knock startled her. She turned to see Jack leaning beside Gramps's window, smiling. She slid the gear back into park, stepped out of the car, and spoke to him over the top. "What are you doing here?"

"Working inside. Saw your car and thought I'd see if you two need help."

"We're okay. I was just thinking..."

But he'd quit listening. He opened Gramps's door, and the two greeted each other like old friends.

It seemed Harper didn't have a choice. And really, had she ever? She couldn't let Gramps starve to death, and without a job—or at least this food bank—that was likely. So, whatever. If she got arrested, she got arrested. She'd survived prison once.

And Gramps? She'd have to trust God to manage him, to manage all of this, because she was out of options.

She pushed the fear aside and grabbed Gramps's walker from the trunk. By the time she had it unfolded, Gramps was standing beside the car. She set the walker in front of him, and they shuffled across the parking lot.

Jack opened the glass door, and she and Gramps stepped onto linoleum floors. There was a reception desk to her right. Beyond that stood fabric-sided cubicles. In one, two people were holding hands across a desk, heads bowed.

In front of her, people of all sorts sat in chairs set in neat rows. Some of the men and women were wrinkled and worn. Others were young and had children in tow. Some were dressed nicely, while others looked as if they'd shopped at Goodwill on a bad day.

There was an older couple taking turns with a toddler, who kept crawling from one lap to the other.

"I'll get Red settled," Jack said. "You go check in."

Harper watched while Jack walked with Gramps to one of the few free chairs before she turned to the desk. Behind it, a woman with long blond hair was typing and staring at a screen. She looked up and regarded Harper with the greenest eyes she'd ever seen. The woman looked young, mid-twenties at most. She was beautiful, but she had a don't-mess-with-me look Harper wished she could perfect. Would that she could be that strong.

"Hi," Harper said. "I heard you have some kind of elderly recreation center."

The woman narrowed her eyes. "You are Jack's renter?"

The question surprised her. "Uh..."

"He told me to expect you." The woman spoke with a slight accent as she handed Harper a clipboard with paperwork. "After you fill this out, bring it back, and I will get you in the system."

The system.

Harper swallowed her apprehension and reached for the clipboard. The instant she had it, the woman focused on the screen again. Harper sat next to Gramps, who'd struck up a conversation with the elderly gentleman beside him. Jack was chatting with a woman behind them while he played peek-a-boo with the toddler in her lap. Harper focused on the paperwork.

Name, address, number of people in her household and their ages, income amount, and source. The income part was easy. Zero. She had to work to keep her hands steady enough to fill out the information. Surely this place wasn't connected to some law enforcement database, right? She squeezed her eyes shut. *Please, God. Please, God. Please protect us. Protect us, heal us, direct us.* Was she asking too much? Was there a limit to what God could—or would—do?

She had to trust. Gramps had been trying to teach her to trust God for months. She was trying, despite everything.

She returned the clipboard to the woman behind the counter,

who took the paperwork with hardly a glance. "Have a seat. Someone will call you back in a minute."

When Harper returned to the chairs, Jack stood. "I'm going to get to work. Red, don't cause too much trouble."

"No promises."

Jack turned that smile on her. As if she didn't feel vulnerable enough. "Good luck. I hope she has some ideas for you."

"You've gone above and beyond," Harper said. "Thank you."

"What are neighbors for?" He walked down a long hallway and disappeared through a door.

She fretted and Gramps chatted with other clients while people disappeared into the cubicles, then continued down the hallway, where they grabbed grocery carts that were lined against the wall. Harper didn't see what happened after that, but she imagined there was a room back there filled with food. Glorious, free food.

With Jack here, she should refuse it. Her landlord didn't need to know the level of her desperation. But her pride was overshadowed by her need. The first month's rent was paid for, and all the utilities were included in the rent. If she could get food, they could survive until she had a paycheck coming in. Maybe, just maybe, she could build a life here in Nutfield. Maybe with her and Gramps out of the way, Derrick would take what he wanted and leave her alone. Maybe nobody would connect her to the two bodies.

No, she couldn't think about that.

The chairs were empty except for her and Gramps when, finally, the blonde came around from the front desk, flipped a sign on the front door to closed, and approached. "You will come with me now." She looked at Gramps. "Sir, do you mind waiting here?"

"Not a bit. Gotta read about my Redskins. Maybe this'll be the year." Gramps focused on the sports page. He wouldn't actually read it—he hadn't done much reading since his memory started to slide. But he'd find a way to keep busy, so Harper stood and followed the woman. They stepped into an empty cubicle, and the woman took a seat behind a desk, where she tapped on a keyboard and focused on the screen. She waved toward a clipboard on the desk. "If you'll sign in."

Harper filled out her name and address and signed it. When she looked up, the woman was watching her with calculating eyes.

"I am Vanessa Baker. I'm the manager here."

"Nice to meet you."

The woman's expression didn't shift from... what was that? Caution? Suspicion? "What brings you to Nutfield?"

"We just needed a change."

"Bah. I don't think so." She waved Harper's words away like an unwelcome smell. "But you don't have to tell me. And your grandfather, he is well?"

Harper was reeling from the woman's words but forced herself to focus. "Usually. He has dementia, which has been getting worse lately. Today is a good day, so far. He also has a bad back that makes it hard for him walk."

"He is in pain, no?"

"He never complains."

"On painkillers?"

"He doesn't like to take them, but sometimes, he has to. When the pain is unbearable."

The woman regarded her with narrowed eyes, mouth pinched. After a moment, she nodded once, said, "Okay," and typed on her computer. "You are looking for a job?"

"Yes. I'll take anything. But Gramps... It would be better if I didn't have to leave him at home alone."

"You have no other family who could take care of him?"

"No. None."

The woman wrote something on a yellow sticky note and handed it across the desk. "Go there, tell Bonnie I sent you. She is looking for someone reliable. You can be reliable?"

"Definitely." Harper looked at the note. *McNeal's, 102 Crystal*

Ave. She'd seen the place driving in this morning, a restaurant just a few blocks from here.

Before she could ask, Vanessa said, "Your grandfather can stay in the rec center during the day when you work. If you work evenings or early mornings, you'll get someone else to help. Maybe Jack."

"Oh, I couldn't ask—"

"You don't have many options, Miss Cloud."

"Harper."

The woman nodded. "Harper, you should also know that your grandfather will be allowed to stay in the rec center because Jack volunteers for us. Usually, it's just for volunteers and their family members."

More favors. More to owe the man. "That's not necessary. I can volunteer, if that's what it takes."

"Very kind but not necessary. Jack has already agreed, so you can focus on getting a job and caring for your grandfather."

"But, I mean..."

For the first time, Vanessa's green eyes filled with warmth. "I understand this fear you carry. None of us wants to owe another person. Especially a man." Her eyebrows lifted, waited.

"Right." How did this woman see so easily into her heart? "It's not easy."

"They are not all..." She waved toward the air, as if words were floating about, waiting to be snatched. "Some are... many are not trustworthy. I have met many of these kinds of men. You have, too, no?"

This woman knew exactly what she was thinking. "Yeah."

"I do not know him well, but from what I do know, Jack Rossi is a nice man, a kind man. So I think it will be okay. If he has any expectations beyond a thank-you"—she pierced Harper with a knowing look—"you tell me, and I'll take care of it. We have to stick together, no?"

Harper let out a surprised laugh. "We do, don't we?"

The woman smiled, and her expression lit the room. Beyond the tough exterior resided a woman Harper would love to know better. But she doubted she ever would. Because to get Vanessa to open up, she'd have to do the same. And there was no way Vanessa or Jack or anybody could know the truth about Harper Cloud.

CHAPTER TEN

Derrick checked his watch again, then compared it with the time on his cell phone. Sure enough, the watch was two minutes behind. Seven thousand dollars for this state-of-the-art timepiece—bought used, though nobody needed to know that—and the piece of crap didn't keep good time.

He needed to sell it. He needed to sell everything he owned, and even that wouldn't be enough.

He glared at the receptionist, whose focus was on her computer screen. She didn't care that Derrick had a job to do. She couldn't care less that his entire life hung from a very thin thread, that if he didn't find his grandfather—fast—he'd lose everything.

Derrick stood, paced across the small room, his gaze hitting and bouncing off all the so-called artwork. Pretty pictures with pretty lies, quotes from a Bible only the most foolish believed. *Trust in the Lord with all your heart...* Right. Like, if only he believed in some invisible God, everything would work out just fine. Derrick knew better. He was the only one who cared about his life and his future. He was the only one willing to fight for it.

The receptionist's phone dinged, and he spun to stare as she answered. A moment later, she set the phone on its cradle. "Go on in. He's ready for you."

"It's about time." Derrick yanked on the ends of his shirt sleeves, smoothed his jacket, and pulled open the door.

Roger Canfield stood behind his huge desk. He wore a dark gray cable-knit sweater and slacks, a far cry from the attire Derrick expected of an attorney. Apparently, when you were still working in your seventies, you could dress however you wanted. Roger extended his hand. "Derrick. Glad you could come in."

Derrick shook his hand and stifled the complaint about the wait. "Thanks for seeing me."

Roger gestured toward the two leather chairs that faced the desk. "Tell me what's going on."

Derrick unbuttoned his suit coat and dropped into the chair. "Harper Cloud, the nurse I hired to take care of Gramps—"

"And your girlfriend, if I remember correctly." Roger settled himself in the huge chair on the other side of the desk, knees creaking with the effort. The desk itself was clear except a telephone, a cell phone, a legal-sized notepad, and a pen. "I met her. She's a lovely person. Devoted to your grandfather."

"She *was* devoted to him, and she *was* my girlfriend. I guess when I broke up with her, she took it harder than I realized."

"What happened?"

"She took him. I went over there Monday, and they were gone. Checked again yesterday. No sign of them."

"So you explained on the phone," Roger said. "And you're sure they didn't take a trip and forget to tell you?"

"She's not answering her phone. And Gramps was sick last week. They're gone, Roger."

"You called the police?"

"Of course." Derrick had had a long conversation with a police officer the day before, asking that a Silver Alert be put out on his grandfather. "Since he's never been diagnosed with dementia or Alzheimer's, they won't do anything."

"Your grandfather is an adult. He has the right to come and go as he pleases."

"But she took him! He would never leave without telling me."

The old man looked past Derrick and nodded slowly. After a moment, he focused his sharp eyes on Derrick again. "Why would she do that? It would be one thing to take off, but why take your grandfather with her?"

"I don't know!" Derrick threw up his hands to emphasize the point. "To get back at me, I guess. To punish me for dumping her."

Roger settled back in his chair, tented his fingers, and waited.

The scrutiny burned, but Derrick forced himself to meet the man's gaze. After a moment, he shifted, adjusted his glasses, and cleared his throat. "I have no idea what's going on in her mind, Roger. But..." He blew out a breath, considered his next words very carefully. "After I started dating her, after I...well, I fell for her. Hard. And then I learned about her past. She's an ex-con." He looked at the floor, tried to school his face with regret, and looked back up. "If I'd known that, I would never have hired her to care for Gramps. That's why I broke up with her. I mean, I probably could have forgiven it, but she lied about it. She didn't tell me until we'd been together for almost a year. I felt betrayed."

"Did you try to convince your grandfather to fire her when you learned about her past?"

Here's where it got tricky. "I should have. I mean, if I'd known before, I'd never have brought her here. But she was so good with Gramps. I didn't want him to let her go until I found somebody else just as good. I should have waited to break up with her, but it seemed wrong to pretend. I tried to be honest with her, above-board." He shook his head, filled his voice with despair. "This is all my fault. I handled it all wrong. And now..." Derrick waited for Roger's response. At this point, the man should tell him it wasn't his fault and offer to help. That's what most people would do.

But Roger Canfield wasn't most people. And no doubt Gramps had told his attorney all about Derrick's life and problems.

"You want me to report the debit card stolen?" Roger asked. "I'm sure you don't want her to have access to his cash."

"No, no. Just keep an eye on it, let me know if she uses it and where. At least that'll be a clue."

Roger nodded. "What do you think she's after?"

"Money, of course. I think she'll call you, beg you to help her. She'll probably have some sorry story. Or..." He paused as if this idea had just occurred to him. "Oh, my God, you don't think she'll make a ransom demand? She has to know what Gramps is worth."

"If she did, would you want to pay it?"

"Of course! I'll do anything to get Gramps back."

Roger made a note on the sheet in front of him. "How much would you be willing to pay?"

"Me?" He feared his true reaction had come through. As if he'd pay a dime for the old man's return. "I don't have the kind of money she'll want, but Gramps's estate could cover it."

"I see." Another notation on the sheet. This one took more time.

What was the man writing? Derrick tried to read the words upside down, but the scrawl was illegible. Roger set the pen down, and Derrick snapped his gaze up.

"If I hear from her," Roger said, "or if there's any activity on the account, I'll certainly let you know." Roger stood. "I trust you'll do the same."

Derrick stood as well. "Of course. In the meantime, I'm hoping to hire a private investigator to help me find them."

"Excellent idea. Do you need some recommendations? I'm sure one of my associates—"

"I've been in contact with someone who comes highly recommended." He adjusted his glasses again, buttoned his jacket. "I will need some help with the retainer, of course."

Roger's smile was tighter than his grip on Gramps's money. "Of course. Have him send me the bill, and I'll take care of it."

"This guy's not with a big firm. It would be faster if you just gave me—"

"I would need your grandfather's go-ahead to transfer the money to you. I have the leeway to pay necessary expenses, but not to give cash payouts."

"Under the circumstances, you could make an exception."

The man's smile was Splenda-sweet, but his eyes were shrewd. "No need. Just have your investigator send me a bill, and I'll be happy to pay it."

Derrick stifled his reaction. "Excellent, then. That'll work. Thank you for your help."

They shook hands, and Derrick left, seething. It was time to cash in a favor.

CHAPTER ELEVEN

Harper followed Vanessa back to the waiting area, where Gramps still sat, alone. He looked up, smiled his most charming smile, and set the newspaper beside him. "Did you get yourself a job?"

"Not yet," Harper said, "but I have a prospect."

"No idea why you want to work," he said, "but it's your life." He looked beyond Harper to Vanessa and struggled to his feet.

Harper had to squeeze her hands into fists to keep from helping him, because he'd certainly bat her arm away. In the six months she'd been caring for Gramps, she'd learned his moods. This was his happy I-don't-need-you mood. Offering to help would offend him.

He made it to his feet and held out his hand to Vanessa. "Harold Burns, but everybody calls me Red, on account of my luxurious red hair."

Vanessa shook his hand. "It is a pleasure."

"Nice accent. You're not from around here, eh?"

"I am from Serbia."

"Never been there. Spent some time in Korea way back. Once I hit American soil, I swore I'd never leave the good old US of A again."

"I can understand," Vanessa said. "I love this country. I hope I will be allowed to stay forever."

"You're not a citizen?"

"I am not, but I'm working on it."

"Well, good for you. Good for you." He focused on Harper again. "Where we going now, girl?"

"Actually," Vanessa said, "I hoped you'd let me introduce you to some of my friends. Can you come with me?" Vanessa turned and started slowly toward the door in the back, the one where Jack had disappeared.

Gramps looked at Harper with narrowed eyes. "You know what's going on?"

Harper shrugged and set the walker in front of him. "Let's find out."

They followed Vanessa down the hall and through the door. On the other side, they found a huge warehouse to their left where people were working and chatting. It was chilly, thanks to the open garage-style door in the back. In the center of the room was a walk-in freezer, if the stainless steel exterior was any indication. A wall stood to their right with a single door and, beyond that, a set of double doors. Harper could see through a glass window into the first, an office.

Vanessa led them to the double doors. These, too, had glass windows, so Harper got a glimpse inside. It seemed like a living room. They stopped just outside the entrance. "Mr. Burns—"

"Red," he corrected with a smile.

Vanessa nodded slightly. "Red, your neighbor Jack has been kind enough to build this room for us. It's a place where our volunteers and their families congregate. I think you'll enjoy it because a lot of our volunteers are near your age. They play cards, watch TV, and generally try to stay out of trouble."

Gramps's charming smile slid off, and he focused on Harper. "What's going on?"

She shrugged as if this were all perfectly normal. "Jack just thought you might like to meet some people."

Before Gramps could argue, Jack appeared in the doorway. "Red. So glad you're here."

Gramps's suspicious expression didn't fall away entirely, but it did slip a little. "You again."

"I'm everywhere."

Gramps peered from Harper to Jack and back as if he were trying to solve a riddle.

"Come on in," Jack said. "I want to introduce you to my friends."

"Well, all right." His frown stayed in place. "If you really want to."

Harper started to follow, but Vanessa stopped her with a hand on her arm. "You give me your cell phone number, and we will call you if there's a problem. They'll keep him entertained until you get back."

"Okay." She touched Gramps on his elbow. "I'll be back in a few minutes."

He nodded and focused on the room. It was designed like a living room. It was warm in here. Six recliners faced a TV mounted on the wall. Two were occupied with gray-headed women. Behind the La-Z-Boys, a game table was surrounded by six padded chairs, and three old men were engrossed in a loud conversation and playing cards. Windows along one wall filled the room with natural light. A few lengths of molding leaned against the wall beside a step ladder. That must have been where Jack was working. Jack would take care of Gramps if he needed anything.

Harper followed Vanessa back into the warehouse, pulled her cell from her purse, and sighed. Two bars here in town. Not great, but at least she had service. She'd had service at the house all day the day before and that morning, too. Maybe it had just been bad on Monday because of the storm. She hoped so. She couldn't afford another phone.

She focused on Vanessa. "If you have a piece of paper—"

"Program my number in your phone. Then, if you need me, you can call."

"Uh... okay." She typed in the phone number as Vanessa rattled it off, then she texted the number with her name. A phone dinged from Vanessa's pocket.

"Good," Vanessa said. "We're set then."

Harper knew it was time to go, but she couldn't quite figure this woman out. "You give all the clients your phone number?"

"Almost none. But you... I think I have been where you are, at least on some level. If not for the kindness of strangers, I do not know where I would be. So, I will be a kind stranger to you."

Oh. Harper had no idea what to say to that.

Vanessa waved her toward the back door of the warehouse. "Go out that way and walk around. The front door is locked. I will take Red to get some food and have it ready when you return. Do either of you have food restrictions or allergies?"

Food. She'd totally forgotten about food. She wanted to hug Vanessa for thinking of it. "He can't eat anything too spicy. And don't let him get all junk food."

"Don't worry. I've done this before." She nodded toward the door. "Good luck with Bonnie." Vanessa stepped into the rec center, where voices and laughter floated out.

Harper headed toward the door. There were people between here and there, volunteers loading shopping bags into waiting cars, others stacking food or sorting produce. This was a big operation for such a small community. She weaved among the people, trading smiles and how-are-yous until she got outside.

Five minutes later, she stepped into McNeal's. The scents of coffee and bacon enticed her. The place had a hometown feel to it, with walls painted sage green and decorated with sports paraphernalia and posters. She grinned at all the Patriots, Red Sox, Celtics, and Bruins stuff and looked more closely at the few framed newspaper articles and banners bragging about the Nutfield Squirrels, apparently the local high school's team, that hung from the wall behind the hostess station. There were TVs in every corner and a very large one on the back wall.

The dark hardwood of the floor matched the long bar. The

walls were lined with booths, and round tables filled the center of the space. Many of the tables were empty, but a few were occupied by folks drinking coffee and enjoying a late breakfast.

A woman came through the door beside the bar that had to lead to the kitchen. She called, "Be right with ya, hon," as she carried plates to the couple seated by the front window.

Harper glanced at a menu. McNeal's served a full breakfast until eleven, then switched to the lunch and dinner menu. Lots of Irish fare—corned beef and cabbage, Reuben sandwiches, shepherd's pie. There were multiple hamburger options, a few steak dinners, chicken—grilled, baked, or fried. They served salads, though not for the health-conscious, if the toppings were any indication.

Comfort food, comfortable surroundings. Harper could see herself working here. It wasn't ideal, but it would keep her bills paid and food on the table.

The waitress headed her way. She was maybe five-foot-two and certainly not in bathing-suit shape. She had short curly brown hair and wore a name tag that read *Bonnie*. "Table for one, hon?"

"Actually, Vanessa sent me. She thought you might have a job for me."

The woman stopped at the hostess station and eyed Harper head to toe. Her lips pinched. The well-worn wrinkles told Harper she'd made that expression before. "You don't look the waitress type."

Harper pushed her hair behind her ears. "What type would that be?"

The woman shrugged. "No offense. It's not like people are banging down the door to work here."

So far, this wasn't going as Harper had imagined. "Is it that bad?"

"Nah. People are just lazy. It's a great job if you know how to work." She gave Harper another once-over. "You look a little bit like a princess, tell you the truth."

"Then think of me as Cinderella before the prince."

The woman cracked a smile, and her whole face changed. "I like the wit. I'm Bonnie Wells." She thrust out her hand, and Harper shook it.

"Harper Cloud."

"Good to meet you. Come on in, and let's have a chat."

Harper followed Bonnie to the back of the room, where Bonnie indicated a chair at the bar. "Sit. I'll be right back." She disappeared into the back, returned with an application and a pen. "Fill this out." After Bonnie rushed away, Harper sat on the wooden barstool and filled out the application. She stopped when she got to the question that would keep her from getting hired.

Have you ever been convicted of a felony?

Her hand hovered over the honest answer, but she didn't check the box.

How could she? If she didn't get a job, she and Gramps would be lost.

She ignored her conscience, shot up a quick *forgive me*, and checked *No*.

As Harper was completing her employment history, Bonnie returned. "You done?"

Harper looked up and smiled. "Just a few more jobs to add."

"Any waitressing experience?"

"Yeah. I worked a cocktail lounge in Vegas." She hadn't done a lot of waiting tables, but she'd done enough for it to qualify. She didn't figure Bonnie would care about her kitchen duty in prison.

"Other jobs you're adding—are they waitressing?"

"No. When I was in high school—"

"We're good then." Bonnie snatched the application and looked it over. "You're a nurse?"

"Used to be."

"So why not get a job doing that?"

"I really need something close by, and fast."

The woman eyed her a moment, and Harper braced for more questions. But all Bonnie said was, "What hours can you work?"

"The lunch shift would be ideal. I care for my grandfather, and he'll need more attention in the evenings and mornings."

"I can't guarantee you'll only get lunch shifts, but we can try. If I can't, can you make arrangements for your grandfather?"

Harper swallowed, smiled. "Sure. I'll work something out."

Bonnie looked over the application, and her eyebrows lifted. "Dancer? What kind of dancer?"

Of course she'd pick up on that one. "The kind you're imagining."

Bonnie leaned back almost imperceptibly. But Harper noticed. Keep your distance from the stripper. She might be diseased.

She imagined how Bonnie would react if she knew the whole truth.

"I don't do that anymore," Harper said. "Believe me, I could make a lot more money if I did."

Bonnie's lips pinched again as she regarded Harper. "I bet you could." She tsked, paused, tsked again. "Lots of women would lie. I appreciate your honesty."

Harper couldn't speak for the sawdust wedged in her throat. Honesty. If she were truly honest, nobody would ever hire her for anything.

But Bonnie didn't pick up on the guilt that felt as solid as the seat beneath her. "Can you start tomorrow?"

CHAPTER TWELVE

J ack finished caulking around the crown molding and returned the ladder to the warehouse. The food bank's clients were gone, and only a few volunteers remained, their keys jingling from fingertips as they finished up conversations.

Vanessa was in her office. Just outside her door stood a shopping cart loaded with food. That must have been what they'd collected for Red and Harper.

Jack returned to the rec center for his tools. Red was seated at the game table with Steve, the father of one of the board members. Ever since Steve had been coming here instead of rattling around his big house alone all day, his health and memory had improved. Amazing what a little companionship could do.

As a member of the board, Jack had been happy to volunteer his services to build this room. His own folks were still going strong, but one day he hoped they'd have somewhere like this to spend time.

"Jack, come over here," Red called from the table. "I need you to prove me right."

"Fat chance, old man." Steve's eyes narrowed as Jack

approached. "You know the movie with Marilyn Monroe and Jack Lemmon?"

"Can't say that I do," Jack said.

"Come on, boy." Red shook his head as if he'd never heard anything so preposterous. "It's called *Some Like it Hot.* 'Course you've seen it."

"That's not the name of it," Steve said. "That was that other movie with Marilyn and Jane Russell."

"No, that's..." Red paused, seemed to be digging through very dusty file cabinets in his mind. "Don't tell me. It'll come to me."

Jack pulled out his cell. "I can figure it out."

The men continued to argue while Jack typed on his keyboard. He got the answer and looked up. "Sorry, Steve. *Some Like it Hot* has Marilyn, Jack Lemmon, and—"

"Tony Curtis," Steve said. "Just like I told you."

Red's eyes bulged. "You said that was that other movie." He snapped his fingers. "*Gentlemen Prefer Blondes.*"

Steve shook his head, though his eyes twinkled. "That's the one with Jane Russell."

"That's what I...!" Red looked at Jack for backup, but Jack just lifted his hands and stepped away. "Not my circus, not my monkeys."

"You just call me a monkey, boy?" Steve said.

"More like an elephant with those ears," Red said.

Steve cupped his dinner-plate sized ear. "What'd you say?"

Red started to repeat himself, then laughed. He banged the table beside him with age-spotted hands. "Sit down, son. Want to join us for a game of cards?"

Jack pulled out the chair and sat. "You guys play without me."

"In my day, a man wouldn't turn down a game of cards." Steve shuffled and shook his head.

Red turned his sharp gaze on Jack. "So, you're in real estate."

"Just dabbling right now, but—"

"Why you dabbling?" Red asked. "Jump in. Real estate's a great investment."

"I know, but there's only so much time. And money."

Red waved off the words. "You don't risk your own money. You gotta find investors, look for houses you can assign to come up with the cash."

Jack rubbed the back of his neck. "Not sure what you mean by that."

Red shot a look at Steve, who was still shuffling cards. "You believe this guy?"

Steve straightened the cards against the table. "You find a property that's going for cheap, get a contract, then turn around and sell it for a little more, a couple thousand. You did the legwork finding the place, so your buyer's happy for the deal. They know you're making money, but if they do it right, they will too. Everybody wins."

Jack's gaze went from one man to the other. "Were you both in real estate?"

"Just a little," Steve said. "I never got into assigning properties, but I always wanted to. Just too busy with the day job. I bought a few multi-families in Manchester back in the eighties. Held on to them, too. In my day, we didn't do all that house flipping like you young people do."

"You said it," Red said. "How'd those buildings work out?"

"Had to weather some storms," Steve said, "but I held onto them. Just sold them a few years back when I retired. The hassle, you know?"

Red nodded. "I still own a few of my properties, but I have a management company taking care of them. It's rough. I have to trust them." He turned his gaze back to Jack. "That's the biggest thing, son. Knowing who you can trust. It's not like it was in my day. Back then, a handshake meant something. People kept their word. These days, most folks'll sell you out for a couple bucks. And not just strangers, either." The light in his eyes dimmed at that, and he focused on the table.

After a beat, Jack said, "Maybe you guys could teach me some stuff. I can use all the help I can get."

Red's gaze snapped up. "Happy to, son. I'll tell you everything I know."

Steve snorted. "Five minutes later, you can come find me."

The men were laughing when the door swung open and Harper stepped in.

Steve whistled. "Who's the looker?"

Harper blushed and focused on her grandfather.

"Did you get the job?" Red asked.

Her smile lit the room as if someone had flipped a switch. "I start tomorrow."

"Well, then." Red pounded the table. "I'm proud of you, girl. And that'll be perfect, 'cause I can come back here and hang out while you're at work."

Harper's glance flicked to Jack.

"Sounds like a good plan," he said. "Let me grab those groceries for you. Did you park out back?"

Ten minutes later, he'd loaded the groceries in Harper's trunk and helped Red to the car. He promised to stop by soon and closed the door. Harper was standing beside the trunk, so he joined her there. "Congratulations on the new job."

"Thanks." She swallowed, seemed to want to say more, so he kept quiet. "Jack, it's been a long time since..." Her voice faded, and she forced a smile, though the tremble he saw on her lower lip told him there was a lot going on behind those beautiful blue eyes. "Your kindness has meant the world to me. I can't even begin to..." She swallowed again.

"All I did was—"

"Bring us dinner, build a ramp, tell us about this place, get them to let Red hang out, help me find a job. Not to mention yesterday, when Gramps was..."

When she didn't finish, he reached out, rested his palm against her arm. Even through her thick jacket, the touch sent a zing all the way to his toes. He pulled his hand away. "It was my pleasure. Truly."

"It's been a long time since anybody's gone out of the way to help me."

He couldn't imagine that. She was sweet and caring and, frankly, drop-dead gorgeous. He figured people would fall all over themselves to help her.

The emotion behind her eyes told a very different story.

"I was happy to do it. And your grandfather promised to teach me about real estate, so I might be hanging around more than you want."

Her eyes lit, and another zing coursed through. Yikes, this woman had an effect on him.

"Gramps invested his savings from his government job and made himself a very wealthy man." As soon as the words were out of her mouth, her face paled. "Of course, that was a long time ago. He doesn't invest anymore."

Except Red had just told Jack he still owned properties—rentals and the big million-dollar home in Maryland.

"Anyway," Harper said, "thanks again. I'd better get home and feed him lunch. He doesn't do well when he's hungry."

Jack watched as Harper pulled away, taking the rest of her story with her.

CHAPTER THIRTEEN

K nowing there was food in the fridge and a job to go to today had been good medicine for Harper. Answered prayers made for a restful night. She felt safe here, safer than she'd felt in a long time. That icky paranoia that had followed her off and on since she'd been released from prison was gone. For now.

While coffee brewed, she showered and tried not to worry about all the things that could go wrong today. Gramps would have to be lucid, willing to take his meds, and eager to go back to the rec center. She'd have to pack him a lunch so he'd have something to eat while she worked, and then he'd have to remember to eat it. Meanwhile, she'd have to learn a new job and get done before the rec center closed at three.

It should work. She'd been told she'd be working ten-thirty to two. But if she had a table that didn't want to leave or if her replacement didn't show up or if Bonnie decided she needed her to stay longer...

She squeezed her eyes shut and rinsed her hair. *You'll have to handle all those ifs, Lord.*

She waited for some reassurance that her day would be as smooth as Gramps's bald head. None came, and she wasn't surprised. It seemed God didn't give a lot of details. She could use a few concrete answers right now. And not just about her day.

Since the storm had passed, her phone had had decent reception at the house. The internet was slow, but it worked. She'd spent the previous afternoon trying to find out what the police knew about those two dead bodies she'd discovered in the living room back in Maryland. One had been Keith Williams, a Baltimore detective. She'd known that already. She'd called 911 from a pay phone right after she and Red had left the house Thursday night, but *The Baltimore Sun* had no information, nor did their little local paper. If the bodies had been discovered in the city, no news might make sense. But two murdered men—one a cop—found in the living room of a mansion near the bay? Surely somebody would pick up that story.

Harper had even checked the TV stations' websites for something, anything. She'd turned up no information whatsoever, no mention of bodies being found, and no mention of missing men.

A week had passed, and there'd been no news.

Obviously, the police were keeping the information secret. But why?

And weren't murders public information? If so, how would they be able to keep a lid on the story?

She'd counted on learning enough to figure out what had happened, who'd killed those men, why they'd been left for her to find, and who they'd worked for. If nothing else, she wanted to know if she was a suspect in their murders.

Instead, she was left in the dark.

After she dried off, brushed out her wet hair, and dressed, she returned to the kitchen, poured herself a cup of coffee, and opened the Bible she'd picked up at Walmart. She wished she'd thought to grab the journal and Bible she kept in her nightstand at Red's house. She'd been keeping a list of thoughts and questions, things to pray about, things to think about. God might not have spoken to her about the circumstances she'd face today, and God might not have given her the information about those two dead bodies, but

He'd made her a lot of promises in this book, and she'd chosen to put her life in His hands. That meant she had to hold onto those promises. God knew she hadn't murdered anybody and would never, ever hurt Gramps. God would vindicate her. She just hoped He'd do it before she landed back in prison.

She'd finished her daily reading when Gramps pushed his walker down the hallway and settled in the chair across from her. "How about some coffee?"

She poured him a cup, watching to see which of his personalities she'd have to deal with today. Happy would be ideal, grumpy she could handle, but confused... that would ruin everything. "What would you like for breakfast?"

He sipped from his mug and set it down slowly. He looked up, met her eyes. She wasn't sure how to interpret the look she saw there. "What are we doing here?"

Crap. "Having breakfast. Eggs and toast, or..."

He pointed his arthritic finger at her. "Not in the kitchen. In this house. Why are we here?"

She still wasn't sure which Gramps had graced her this morning, but at least he seemed lucid. The problem was, he didn't remember the bodies and had no idea what Derrick had been up to. She wasn't about to tell him. It was all so murky. If she told him what she did know, she had no idea how he'd react. But she couldn't afford for him to demand to go home and straighten it out. He trusted law enforcement. She'd tried that once and paid dearly for her mistake. She wouldn't let Gramps get pulled into that minefield.

She sat and leaned across the table toward him. "Remember I told you we had to get away."

"I don't remember why."

She'd told him an elaborate lie, which he'd bought because he trusted her. She took a deep breath, let the lie come back. "There are people after me, and I had to run. People from my old life. You remember, I told you about my old life."

"I remember."

"I couldn't bear to be away from you, so you decided to come with me."

"Decided?" He narrowed his eyes, met her gaze, and held it. "Don't remember being given a choice."

He'd been so out of it that night, he didn't remember anything.

"I'm sorry, Gramps."

"And that's another thing. Why do you call me that?"

"We decided it would be easier if everybody thought we were related. That way, if you have any health issues, people will naturally come to me."

"You're my nurse. Surely you brought that paper that gives you authority over my healthcare, right? Of course they'd come to you."

"I brought it, but it's so much simpler if everyone thinks we're family. We are family, aren't we?"

He harrumphed. "You're better than that grandson of mine. What did Derrick think of you taking me away?"

She stood and pulled the bread from the drawer. "Oh, Derrick was okay with it. He knows how close you and I have become."

"And you two aren't going to get back together?"

"Definitely not." She turned to meet Gramps's eyes. "But that doesn't change my relationship with you. You know that, right? You're the only real family I've got, and I'll do anything for you."

They held each other's gazes for a long time. She worried he was seeing all the lies in her eyes, but after a moment, he nodded. "If this is what you need to do to be safe, then I'm with you."

She released a breath. "Thank you."

"Just wish I had a picture of my Bebe."

Of all the things to have forgotten. "I'm so sorry."

"Maybe Roger could mail us a copy. He's got a key to the house, and he won't tell anyone where we are."

"That's an idea." One she wouldn't use.

Red sipped his coffee. "I would like to talk to Derrick, though. Can we call him now?"

She busied herself at the fridge, trying to avoid eye contact. "It's awfully early."

"We gotta catch him off guard."

"Probably true." She went to her bedroom, grabbed her phone, and returned to the kitchen, where she checked the service. Three bars. She shook her head sadly. "We don't have service again. We're going to have to get a better cell phone plan."

Gramps shook his head. "Not safe to be without a phone. Why don't we call the phone company, get the kind that plugs into the wall instead of that thing?"

"Good idea. I'll make the call today." And probably discover it was way too expensive, but if it got Gramps's mind off Derrick...

"We'll try him later," Gramps said. "And I'll call Roger, too. Have him wire us some cash. I don't understand why you think you have to get a job."

Gramps wanted to make calls. She hated to pray for memory loss, but he really needed to forget those ideas. She popped two pieces of toast in the toaster. "I don't mind working."

"I guess you don't want to spend all your days with a grouchy old man."

She turned again, shook her head. "Don't say that about yourself. You're not old."

When he got her joke, he laughed. "Ornery girl. Make me some eggs, would ya?"

One crisis had been averted, *thank You, God*, but it was barely seven a.m. She prayed the rest of the day would go as well.

WITH TEN THOUSAND things to remember, she'd never keep them all straight. Harper had thought studying to be a nurse was hard, but that had nothing on waitressing at McNeal's.

When she smiled at the cook, he only scowled at her. The middle-aged man had hardly said two words to her since she'd been there. Now, she set two orders on an oversize tray and headed for the dining room, stopping at the table in front of the windows.

"Baked potato soup for you"—she slid the bowl in front of the pretty woman—"and a steak for you."

The man nodded.

"Thanks so much." The woman had a Southern accent with the manners to match. "You new here?"

"My first day," Harper said.

"New in town, too?"

"Just moved here."

"Welcome." The woman's smile was wide. "This town'll make you feel like you're home. Sure did me, anyway."

It had been so long since Harper felt at home, she didn't know if she'd recognize the sensation. "So far, it's been wonderful."

"Don't let Bonnie give you any flack," the man said with a wink. His accent was Southern, too, though not the same as his wife's. More Texas and less twang. "That woman's got all the charm of a rattlesnake."

"I heard that."

Harper jumped at Bonnie's voice just inches behind her.

"Don't listen to Eric," Bonnie said. "That man lies a like dog. I don't know how Kelsey puts up with him."

Harper smiled at the couple and headed back to the kitchen. So far, the customers had been nice, patient with her when she'd made mistakes. And Bonnie was tough, no doubt, but also kind. A good teacher. Harper could do this job. Based on the tips she'd already collected, she might even be able to support herself and Gramps with it.

Maybe.

It was nearly two when Jack walked in and scanned the restaurant. She was about to head toward him, but he waved her off and crossed the dining room, where he sat across from a gorgeous brunette at one of Bonnie's tables.

Harper tried to shake off the sadness that settled on her shoulders. What in the world did she have to feel sad about? Jack was only a friend, and that was all he could ever be. Apparently, some foolish corner of her heart had hoped for more.

She checked on her tables, refilled a few glasses, and returned to the kitchen for her last party's food, all while trying to push away the image of Jack with the brunette.

Wow, she was a fool. When would she learn not to give her heart away? Every single man she'd cared for had burned her, badly. One had landed her in prison. And Derrick? It was thanks to him she was in hiding. Yet the first guy who showed her a little kindness, and she was falling for him.

Idiot.

Idiot, idiot, idiot.

"Whatcha doing, just standing there?"

She jumped at her boss's voice. "Making sure I didn't forget anything."

"You're doing a good job. Get those meals delivered, and you might even get out of here on time."

Harper returned to the dining room. She served the meals, ran a credit card for a party of four, and was giving the check to another table when she glanced at Jack. He waved her over.

She pasted on a smile and joined him. "Good to see you," she said.

"Harper, I'd like you to meet my real estate agent, Ginny Lamont."

Harper turned to the woman. Yup, she was gorgeous. Dark brown hair, bright blue eyes, wide smile. She held out her hand. "You're the new tenant?"

Harper shook her hand. "Just moved here."

"Welcome."

Jack said, "I saw Red this morning, and he seemed to be having a good time. Steve's there, of course."

"That's good news," Harper said. "I've been worried. Did you have more work to do there?"

"I was in the neighborhood and thought I'd check on him."

Jack had done that just because? What was with this guy?

"I was hoping to grill him about his real estate business," Jack continued. "Ginny's looking for more rentals for me, but Red suggested something else yesterday, and I hoped I'd get more information."

"I'm sure he gave you an earful," she said.

"Nope. He was too engrossed in his poker game."

"Please tell me he wasn't gambling."

"Just pennies, which somebody else supplied. I thought maybe you'd let me bring you guys dinner tonight."

Harper couldn't help the way her gaze darted to Ginny. The woman's smile was still there, tight as a fitted sheet over her gritted teeth. Harper glanced back at Jack, who seemed utterly clueless.

Maybe he didn't care.

Or maybe he liked making her jealous.

"Red said it was fine," Jack said, "but I figured I'd better tell you so you don't fix something. You'll be exhausted after your day."

"Uh..."

"I'll be there about five with lasagna. Your grandfather says it's his favorite."

"It is, but—"

"Excuse me." A customer from another table was waving her over.

Harper just nodded and turned away. She had to focus on work right now. Later, she'd worry about Jack and his suspicious kindness... and Ms. Realtor's angry eyes.

CHAPTER FOURTEEN

Derrick leaned against a wall in his old friend's shabby office. The furniture was generic, the beige walls bare, the carpet one step up from indoor-outdoor and stained in multiple places. The room smelled like stale cigarette smoke along with the bathroom odors from the hall right outside the door.

To say this wasn't the best part of Baltimore would be an understatement. This guy was way outside the circles Derrick usually traveled in. The other businesses in this building included an attorney who specialized in DUI cases, a bail bondsman, and a woman who read tarot cards.

"Seriously," Tank said. "Could you sit? I'm trying to work." Tim *Tank* Anker eyed him from the faux-leather chair behind his worn desk, which was piled high with files and papers and pens and who knew what else. He grabbed his head with his sausage-link fingers, turned it to the side, and cracked his thick neck. Apparently, being a professional private investigator hadn't changed the man too much.

"Check again," Derrick said. "See if he's paid."

Tank blew out a loud breath. "When I get an email, it dings. You hear a ding?"

"Just check."

Tank clicked, looked at his screen. "Nothing. Just let me call you when it comes in."

Derrick wasn't leaving Tank until he had the money. He couldn't. He'd called the night before and explained what he needed. After a long and tense discussion, Tank had sent the invoice to Roger, but by the time he had, Roger had left the office for the day.

Last night at his condo, Derrick had gotten a visit from two of Quentin's goons. Not Keith and his sadistic buddy, which surprised him, but two new guys. They'd given him twenty-four hours to produce "a substantial portion" of what Derrick owed him.

With his checking account having dwindled to pennies, he didn't have enough to pay his electric bill, much less *a substantial portion* of two hundred thousand dollars.

He was in deep trouble this time. He'd called in to work that morning, feigning the flu, so he could find Harper and his grandfather. His boss, a man who saw everything in the same shade of green as a dollar bill, hadn't been pleased. Join the club. Derrick couldn't afford to be away and didn't want to think about all the money he was losing by handing his clients off to another broker. What was that expression? The tyranny of the urgent? In this case, it was the tyranny of the tyrants. If Derrick didn't get his hands on some cash, fast, he would lose everything—including his life.

So here he was, first thing Thursday morning. Who cared that the office was shabby? With Tank he was safe. There weren't a lot of guys willing to take on a man like him. This wasn't college anymore, and Tank wasn't the starting fullback on the football team. And sure, what once had been nothing but muscles born of steroids and hours in the gym was now shrouded in fat and encased in an oversize suit and tie. Still, only a half-wit would take Tank on.

And the guys watching Derrick weren't half-wits.

"I'll wait."

Tank stood and grabbed a Mr. Pibb from the mini-fridge behind his desk. "Want one?"

"You still drink that swill?"

"You used to love it."

"I'm not in college anymore."

Tank popped the top, downed half the soda, and set it on his desk. "When did you get to be such a snob?"

Derrick ignored the question. He and Tank had gone their separate ways after their senior year. After the incident they never talked about.

He leaned against the wall and pulled out his cell, then navigated to his email and answered the latest ones.

Tank lowered himself into his chair, which responded to his weight with a high-pitched gasp. He pointed to the chair across from his desk. "If you're gonna stay in here, you gotta sit. You're making me nuts."

Derrick swallowed his retort, slid his phone back into his jacket pocket, and sat.

Tank steepled his fat fingers. "Tell me what's going on."

"My grandfather's missing. His nurse took him."

"That much you said, and so did that lawyer when we talked this morning. Any ideas where they might be?"

So Roger had called Tank to check on Derrick's story. He shouldn't have been surprised. "I have a couple."

"But you don't want me to find them."

"I can find them. I just need cash."

Tank looked at his computer screen. When he trained his gaze on Derrick again, his eyes were narrowed. "Lotta cash."

"It's none of your business."

Tank leaned back, sat straighter. "Heck it isn't. You call me demanding I make like your PI to funnel cash to you—that makes it my business. And if you really wanna find them, just let me do my job. I'm good at it."

Derrick made a show of looking around the shabby office. "I can see how successful you've been."

Tank dropped his hands to the desk and pressed. His knuckles turned white.

Derrick swallowed hard as he leaned against the back of his chair. He'd seen Tank lose his temper before, and he didn't need to be on the receiving end of that. He started to backpedal, but Tank spoke first.

"Don't jump to a bunch of conclusions, old *friend*." He took a deep breath, and, surprisingly, seemed to rein in his temper. Tank must have picked up a new skill in the years since college. "I like my office. The rent is cheap, and unlike you, I'm not trying to impress anybody. I don't need to. You know why? 'Cause I'm good at what I do. I got a wife now and two kids. So my money goes to support them, not to impress stuck-up suits."

"Okay, okay." Derrick lifted his hands in surrender. "I'm just saying, this isn't the most impressive place to entertain clients."

"I don't meet my clients here. I either go to them or meet 'em at the coffee shop on the corner. You're the one who insisted we meet here, remember?"

Derrick had needed privacy, and to be away from his normal routine. He pushed his glasses up the bridge of his nose. "I'm sorry. It's been stressful with my grandfather missing."

Tank didn't look a bit moved. "I can find him faster than you can."

Derrick didn't know if that was true, and he wasn't about to find out. He didn't want anyone to find them before he did. Not PIs, not lawyers, and not cops. He'd called them in a panic, but he'd been relieved to learn they wouldn't search for Gramps. Better if they stayed far away.

If only Harper had just kept feeding Gramps the Gatorade. Gramps would be out of his misery, reunited with Gram, and Derrick would have the money he needed. Then, if Harper had been lucky, Derrick might have taken her back, given her a second chance. But after this stunt, no way.

"Dude, what do you think?" Tank said. "Just lemme—"

"If I can't locate them in a few days, I'll bring you in. But I have some leads."

Tank drummed his fingers on the desk. He didn't look happy.

The computer dinged. "He sent it."

A twinge of relief settled in Derrick's stomach. "Good. Excellent."

"I'm gonna have to pay tax on this money, man."

"Tax?" Derrick stood, rested his hands on the desk, and leaned forward. "Imagine what you'd have paid back in college if not for me."

Tank stood, too. "I know what you did for me. I don't even know..." He shook his head, stared out the window to the dingy street beyond. "Sometimes I think it would have been better if I'd just done my time, you know?"

"And gone to prison? That what you wanted? To be an ex-con? 'Cause I know a few of those, and life isn't easy after prison."

"I'm not saying that." Tank sat again and stared at the desk. Finally, he looked up. For the first time in...ever, Derrick saw genuine regret in the man's eyes. "What I did to her...it was awful. I shoulda gone to jail for it. That night haunts me. And 'cause you lied for me, I can't ever come clean. Can't tell Emily the truth. Can't tell anybody the truth. I just gotta live this...this lie."

Derrick made a show of taking out his phone. "I can fix that for you right now. Emily? That's your wife? Give me her number, and I'll tell her all the gory details. I'll tell her how you followed your girlfriend out of our apartment that night. How you offered to walk her home, to 'keep her safe.'" He made air quotes around the words. "And how, when you got to her apartment, you forced your way inside, ripped off her clothes, and—"

"Stop!" Tank hid his face behind his hands.

"What? You don't think Emily wants to hear it from me? That's fine. I'll just call the newspapers. Maybe nobody can throw you in jail for it now—you made that fine deal—but the press can destroy your business. I'll tell them how you threatened me, made me lie for you."

"That's a lie. I never asked—"

"*After witness tells all, former fullback finally fesses up.* I like the alliteration, don't you?"

Tank dropped his hands, glared. "You made your point."

"What, you don't want the world to know?" Derrick paced to the back wall and leaned against it. "I thought the guilt was killing you."

"Just…" He waved his Frisbee-sized hand toward the chair.

Satisfied, Derrick sat again.

Tank focused on his computer, tapped a few buttons, and turned to Derrick. "Here's what's gonna happen. You and me, we're gonna go to the bank. I'm gonna get you the cash, and then you're gonna walk away. What we're doing here, it's illegal, and you're just as involved as I am. This ever comes back to bite me, and I'll tell 'em everything. Now, I got something on you, and you got something on me. Got it?"

"As long as our friendship's still intact."

The expletive-laden retort suggested the friendship was off.

CHAPTER FIFTEEN

With a grocery sack hanging from his wrist, Jack carried the pan of lasagna next door. His stomach rumbled with the scents of tomatoes and garlic and sausage as steam rose and mixed with the cold November air.

He had no idea why he was here.

What in the world had prompted him to offer to bring dinner to Harper and Red tonight? Sure, he wanted to talk to Red about real estate. The man seemed to know his stuff. But Jack could easily have stopped by earlier to do that. Besides, he'd had better things to do than spend an hour in the kitchen putting this meal together.

He climbed the ramp and knocked on the door with his foot.

Harper greeted him with a smile. "That smells delicious." She stepped out of his way, and he headed for the kitchen.

"Hey, Red."

The old man lifted his hand in greeting without taking his eyes off the TV.

Harper folded a dishtowel and rested it in the middle of the kitchen table. "Just set it there."

He did and took the foil off the top. "We'd better let it cool before we dig in."

She eyed the concoction with lifted eyebrows. She'd changed out of her jeans and now wore yoga pants and a sweatshirt the way a runway model would wear yoga pants and a sweatshirt. He flashed back to the sight of her in those ridiculous pajamas, and his cheeks warmed. Did this woman ever not look gorgeous?

"You *made* this?"

He laughed at the awe in her voice. "Surprised?"

"When you said lasagna, I just assumed you'd warm up one of those frozen ones. But that's not a disposable pan."

"We Rossis know Italian food."

She inhaled slowly. "I should say so." She turned, pulled three plates from the cabinet, and set them on the table. "You like to cook?"

Jack slid the plates to their spots in front of the chairs. "It's a hobby. Unfortunately, I rarely have anybody to cook for."

Harper opened the silverware drawer. "I bet Ginny would love to sample your masterpieces."

"My real estate agent?" He grabbed some napkins, folded them, and set them beside the plates.

Harper turned, lifted her eyebrows.

"Our relationship is nothing like that."

She turned back to the drawer and took her time pulling out the utensils. "If you say so."

"Besides, she's not my type."

Harper set the forks and knives on the table. "What type is she?"

"I don't know. She's a great real estate agent. But she's from California, and she has some weird ideas." He grabbed the sack he'd carried in, grateful for something to do besides explain to this beautiful woman why another beautiful woman didn't appeal to him. "Salad. Just Caesar. You have a bowl, or should we just serve ourselves from the bag?"

"The bag works." She crossed her arms. "So, tell me about poor Ginny and why being from California is a turnoff."

He shrugged. "Today she suggested that I should spend time

every day visualizing the future I desire and the types of properties I want to buy. She said if I did that, then the universe"—he put air quotes around the word—"would work with me to get me what I wanted."

"Wow." Harper laughed, shook her head. "So have you tried it?"

Behind Jack, Gramps said, "That's just New Age mumbo jumbo."

Jack stepped out of his way. "I agree."

Gramps shuffled through the kitchen behind his walker and sat. "The universe. Pfft. You need something, you ask God. You start making requests of *the universe*, and who the heck knows who's gonna answer." He eyed the pan on the table. "Well, we gonna eat or what?"

"Give me a sec, Gramps." Harper focused on Jack. "I have sweet tea, water, or coffee."

"Sweet tea, huh? Y'all aren't from around here, are you?"

Harper rewarded his fake Southern accent with a laugh. "You want to try it?"

"Why not."

She poured two glasses of iced tea and refilled Red's Gatorade before she settled between him and Red.

Red set his hands palms-up on the table. Harper slid her hand into his and glanced at Jack. He grabbed the old man's hand before taking Harper's. That's when he realized why he'd made the lasagna for them.

An hour of work just to hold a pretty girl's hand. He'd think about how pathetic that was later. Right now, he had to focus on Red's prayer and not on the delicate fingers resting snugly against his palm.

He must've failed, because Harper's amen startled him. Reluctantly, he let her go.

He forced himself to drink the tea, though it was sweeter than rock candy, while he watched Harper and Red savor the meal. What wasn't to like? Homemade spaghetti sauce, hot Italian sausage, three kinds of cheese. But it was Harper's little moans of pleasure that brought him the most joy. And maybe some other emotions he chose not to name.

"You cooked this, boy?"

Jack set his fork on the plate. "My mother's recipe."

"Your mother's a genius." Red forked another bite. "A veritable genius."

"I'll tell her you approve."

Harper set her tea down. "Your folks live around here?"

"I grew up about an hour from here, in Nashua. They still live in the same house."

"What brought you to Nutfield?" Harper asked.

"After college, I got a job working for a real estate management company here. I figured I'd just stay a year or so, get some experience. But I like it here. Nothing wrong with Nashua, but the traffic, the busyness—it's just not me. I prefer small-town life."

Red said, "I like it here, all these trees, all this quiet. Makes a man feel close to God."

The look Harper gave her grandfather was filled with such affection, Jack felt like an intruder. She reached across the table, rested her delicate hand on his gnarled one. "I'm so glad you like it."

He harrumphed and forked another bite of lasagna.

Whatever was going on with these two—and Jack was sure something wasn't right—it was clear they loved each other. And for a woman to do all Harper was doing to take care of her grandfather —that kind of love covered a multitude of sins.

After the meal, Harper gathered their dirty dishes and turned to the sink.

Jack focused on Red. "You said something about assigning properties yesterday. I looked it up online, so I know a little about it. Can you tell me more?"

Red's crinkly eyes narrowed, and he regarded Jack like he might a poisonous snake. "What are you talking about?"

"Uh..." He glanced at Harper, but her focus was on the dishes.

"At the rec center yesterday, you mentioned that you used to assign real estate to protect your own money. Right?"

"Don't know what you're on about, boy!"

At the sound of Red's raised voice, Harper turned, eyes wide.

Jack leaned back, lifted his hands in surrender. "I'm sorry. I must have misunderstood."

Red looked at Harper. "What is he talking about?"

She turned off the water, dried her hands on a towel, and walked to the table. "It's okay. Jack's a friend. He brought us this lovely dinner."

Red eyed the pan of lasagna in the center of the table, seemed to study the pasta still there, the empty place where they'd cut away their slices, the sauce and cheese and sausage that had oozed into that empty place. "I don't like lasagna."

Harper glanced at Jack, then took Red's hand. "That's okay. You already ate anyway. You want to watch some TV?"

Red glanced at her, glared at Jack, and nodded once. "Don't know what I'm doing at this table, anyway. Is Wheel of Fortune on yet? I never miss Wheel of Fortune."

Harper pulled his walker close and helped him stand. Together, they shuffled into the living room while Jack sat at the table uselessly.

A moment later, Harper returned. "Sorry about that. Considering the day he had, the week we've had, I'm amazed he was lucid as long as he was today."

"I didn't mean to upset him."

"It wasn't your fault."

She returned her focus to the dishes.

He wrapped the aluminum foil back over the lasagna and slid it into the fridge.

When he closed the door, he caught her watching him over her shoulder. "You aren't leaving that, are you?"

"You guys can have it. I made a second pan for myself and put it in my freezer to enjoy later."

She turned back to the sink, her head shaking. "Wish I could cook."

"You don't?"

"I can make eggs. I can bake a can of biscuits without burning them. I've perfected the art of tomato soup and grilled cheese."

"How do you survive?"

She set the last plate on the towel she'd laid out and turned to him. "I just told you. Eggs, canned biscuits, tomato soup, and grilled cheese. And... let's see. There's boxed macaroni and cheese, and I can fry those hamburgers you buy in bulk."

"Please tell me you don't mean those frozen things that come already made into perfectly round patties."

She shrugged. "Ground beef is gross. I'm not touching it to make patties."

He shook his head and laughed. "What else?"

"Spaghetti."

"With jarred sauce?"

"It works. Doesn't taste like that, though." She gestured to the fridge and the lasagna he'd stowed there.

"You're killing me."

Her smile made his full stomach do a flip.

She grabbed the sponge to wipe the table.

"Did your mom or dad cook?"

"Mom did," Harper said. "She was a great cook."

"Was? Is she—?"

"Oh, I'm sure she's still a great cook."

Harper turned to wipe down the counters, which were already perfectly clean, while he let her words process. The way she'd answered made him wonder...

"When was the last time you saw her?" he asked.

Harper scrubbed the already clean surface. "It's been a while."

"Is she Red's daughter?"

She turned, looked confused. "Oh. Uh, no. Gramps is on the other side of the family." She tossed the sponge into the sink, passed Jack, and poked her head into the living room. He could just make out Red's soft snores over the sound of the TV.

She returned. "Well, I'd better start getting him ready for bed."

Bed? It was just after six.

She leaned against the door jamb and crossed her arms. "He's had a long day, and so have I. Thanks for dinner."

A not-so-subtle hint even Jack could pick up on. He walked to the front door. "Thanks for the hospitality."

She barely cracked a smile. "Sure. Anytime."

If *anytime* meant *never again*, he might believe her.

On the short walk home, he thought about what had just happened. Everything had been going just fine until he'd asked about her family. Then, her countenance had snapped shut like a trap door.

He couldn't help but wonder what was beyond that door.

CHAPTER SIXTEEN

Harper couldn't believe the crowd. For some reason, she'd thought Monday would be slow at McNeal's. One more thing she'd been wrong about.

She'd really blown the *keep her head down* portion of her plan the week before. What had she been thinking, asking Jack about his family? Of course he'd reciprocate and ask about hers. She couldn't tell him the truth. And she was a lousy liar. What choice had she had but to send him away before he asked more questions?

His expression still haunted her. She'd insulted him. Apparently, she'd insulted him a lot, because she hadn't seen him since. In fact, if she weren't mistaken, he'd gone out of his way to avoid her. When she and Gramps had returned to the house on Friday afternoon, she'd seen that Jack had been there to rake up the last of the leaves in the front yard. She could picture him now, watching from his house next door until their car drove away, then rushing over to get it done while they were gone.

That's how rude she'd been Thursday night.

She'd thought surely she'd see him over the weekend, be able to offer her thanks, maybe even an apology. It was probably better she hadn't, because an apology might lead to more questions she couldn't answer. It would be better if she kept her distance from

Jack and Bonnie and everybody else she had contact with. If they knew the truth, they'd reject her.

Except Gramps, who knew everything and loved her anyway.

Everything she was doing, all she'd lost—it would all be worth it if she could only keep Gramps safe.

She managed to finish her shift in time—barely. The rec center would close in ten minutes, so she hung up her apron, waved to Bonnie, and headed for her car. On her way, she checked her phone and discovered she'd missed a phone call.

She swiped it on, looked again to make sure she wasn't crazy. She'd missed four phone calls.

Crap, crap, crap.

While she drove toward the food bank, she listened to the first message. Vanessa's voice, her no-nonsense tone and Serbian accent. "Your grandfather is very confused, and he is getting agitated. Please call us immediately."

In the food bank's lot, she jammed the car into *Park* and ran in the back door. The warehouse was empty.

Steve, the older man she'd met the other day, was just coming out of the rec center.

He saw her, shook his head. "Your grandfather isn't here."

Her shock must've shown on her face, because he patted her arm with his age-spotted hand. "He's okay. He got confused and—"

"I called you."

Harper turned to see Vanessa coming from her office.

"I'm sorry. My phone has terrible reception. Where is Gramps?"

"He was not able to be calmed," Vanessa said.

"He was ticked off," Steve added.

Harper turned back to Vanessa, who said, "I called Jack. He took him home."

Jack. She closed her eyes, felt the tears burning. Poor Gramps. He must have been terrified. And she'd had no idea.

A hand squeezed her shoulder. She opened her eyes and smiled at Steve, who patted her arm awkwardly. "It'll be okay."

"You need a new phone," Vanessa said.

"Yes. I'll... It won't happen again."

Vanessa nodded once, spun, and returned to her office.

Steve let his arm drop and tilted his head toward the door where Vanessa had just disappeared. "She was worried. I don't know her very well. Nobody does, to tell you the truth. But from what I can tell, she masks every emotion with irritation."

Harper focused on the old man. "If you say so."

"She'll get over it."

She'd better, because without this place, Harper wouldn't be able to keep her job. And then what would she and Gramps do?

CHAPTER SEVENTEEN

J ack settled on the sofa in Red's house and exhaled a long breath.

Vanessa had called him when she couldn't get in touch with Harper. He'd left the work he was doing at one of the cabins he managed and rushed into town. He'd thought to stop at McNeal's to tell Harper what was going on, but he figured he'd better check on Red first.

Once he had Red in his pickup, there was no leaving him alone. The old man beside him bore no resemblance to the Red that Jack had come to know. He was angry, aggressive, and irrational. This was the man who'd caused that gash on Harper's temple almost a week earlier. It took all of Jack's focus to keep him from diving out of the pickup and hurting himself.

Jack had considered taking Red home with him, but Red had never been to his house, and Jack hoped maybe the familiarity of his own living room might help calm him down. So he'd used his spare key, let himself into Red and Harper's house, and then cajoled the angry old man up the ramp and into his chair.

Red had complained and yelled and fought him every step.

It wasn't until Jack turned on the TV and found a soap opera that Red settled down. Jack made him a sandwich, encouraged him to eat it, and managed to get him to drink half a glass of Gatorade. He had no idea if food or hydration would help, but they couldn't hurt.

Jack was way out of his league here.

He'd planned to call the restaurant and ask for Harper as soon as he had a free moment. But by the time he got Red calmed down enough to do so, he was so angry, he couldn't think straight. Why hadn't she answered Vanessa's calls? Did she really intend to leave her grandfather for others to care for? She hadn't seemed that type of woman, but after Thursday... Well, clearly he had no idea what type of woman she was.

Rude, no doubt about that. Secretive. And, if Thursday night's conversation could be believed, estranged from her family. A family that could have helped her with Red. Seemed to Jack that if she really cared about the old man, she'd mend whatever fences she'd torn down with them.

After Red had finished the sandwich, he'd focused on the TV. Now, he was snoring softly, his head lolling to the side.

Finally, he heard a car in the driveway. A moment later, Harper burst through the front door. She looked at the old man and grabbed the door jamb. "Thank God."

Jack's anger slipped a few notches. With a nod toward the kitchen, he whispered, "Come on."

She collapsed on a chair and dropped her head into her hands. "I'm so sorry. My phone... I don't know what happened."

Tears dripped between her fingers and landed on her lap.

He'd seen her phone. It looked like a cheapie one might buy in a convenience store. No wonder it didn't work. He leaned against the counter and crossed his arms. "You need to replace that phone."

She reached for a napkin, wiped her eyes, took a deep breath. "As soon as I get my first paycheck." More tears dripped, and she wiped them away, focusing on her lap. "Why didn't Vanessa call me at McNeal's?"

He'd wondered the same thing. "Maybe because she knows it's

your first week there. Maybe she didn't want to jeopardize your job. And she figures we're friends."

Her gaze snapped up and met his. She swallowed, blinked away fresh tears. "I'm sorry I was so rude last week. I just... My family is a hard topic."

"I gathered."

She straightened her shoulders, took another deep breath, seemed to be steeling herself. "What happened with Gramps?"

"According to Steve, he was fine. And then he wasn't. I figure it was sort of like what happened the other night. Except nobody there knew how to handle it."

"Sometimes I can't handle it, either. You saw him last week."

"Do you think it's Alzheimer's?"

She shrugged. "It's just been in the last month or so that he's gotten aggressive." She paused, took a breath. "To be honest, he's actually better than he was a few weeks back. His memory was failing a little, yes, but for a while, he was angry and confused much more than he has been here." She turned toward the doorway and her sleeping grandfather.

Jack surveyed the kitchen, the dingy house he'd rented them. He weighed his next words carefully, figured he was about to get thrown out again. But it had to be said. "Wouldn't he do better in his own home?"

She deflated like a balloon with a fast leak. "You don't understand."

"Explain it to me."

She pressed her hands together, stared at the cabinets.

He lowered his voice, tried to sound gentle. "If you took him home to your family, would they take care of him?"

She didn't answer, but fresh tears dripped down her cheeks.

"You don't think your father, Red's own son, would help you?"

"You don't understand."

"So you said."

She stood, opened the fridge, pulled out a package of American cheese. Well, those nasty individually-wrapped orange squares people tried to pass off as cheese. She unwrapped it, nibbled the edge like a frightened mouse.

"Have you eaten?" he asked.

She shook her head, focused on the floor.

He edged by her, opened the fridge again, and pulled out the pan of lasagna. Only one serving remained. "How about I warm this up for you?"

"I can feed myself."

He just lifted his eyebrows and waited.

She took the pan from him, cut the small portion in half, and put it on a plate. "You want some?"

"There's barely enough for one."

She glanced at the portion she'd dished herself. "I won't eat more than that."

He'd had a sandwich with Red, but the lasagna looked good. When he said nothing else, she took the rest, put it on a second plate.

While the food heated in the microwave, she washed the empty pan and set it on the table. Then she got them both glasses.

"Water for me," he said.

She filled two glasses and grabbed their meals.

They ate with only the sound of the soap opera in the other room and their forks against the dishes for noise.

When he finished, he stood with his empty plate. "You about to kick me out again?"

"I didn't kick you out. I just..."

When she didn't finish, he turned to the sink to rinse the empty dish.

"Just leave it."

"And go," he added, figuring that's what she wanted.

She gestured toward the other chair. "Unless you need to go. You probably have work to do or something. I'm sure we messed up your day."

He sat. "I'm good."

Her plate was still half-full when she pushed it away. "I don't have a relationship with my parents. I want to. Maybe someday I'll have the nerve to go home, but not yet."

"Why?"

"Why what?"

It was like trying to question a hostile witness. He'd have made a terrible lawyer. "Why don't you have a relationship with them?"

"They were good parents. Raised me with love. Taught me right from wrong. I chose wrong."

Vague, but getting somewhere. "How so?"

She sipped her water, set it down. Folded her hands. They were trembling. "After I graduated from high school, I took off. Decided I wanted to be an actress."

"They didn't like that idea?"

"They were very supportive. I got a job in Hollywood as a barista, auditioned for every role I could. At one of them, I met this guy. He offered me a job dancing in a show in Vegas. It wasn't Hollywood, but it was a paying job. I was thrilled."

Her wry smile told him the thrill had worn off quickly.

"The job was fine. The guy and I started dating. And then we had a falling out." The way her lip ticked up at the corner, a look of pure disgust, made him wonder. "He kicked me out of his apartment, and I got fired from the job."

"Because you dumped him?" A rush of anger had the words out before he could stop them.

"Apparently, sleeping with him was one of my job requirements. I hadn't realized..."

The lasagna turned in his stomach. "I'm sorry."

"I should have gone home. But I'd made this big deal about how I was going to make it in show business, not just to my family but to everyone. To old friends who'd gone off to college and gotten real jobs. I was embarrassed." She sipped her water. "I knew people. I had work experience. I thought I could get another job."

Her gaze darted around the room as if collecting words, trying to put them together. "But that guy, the one from before... He'd introduced me to drugs." She swallowed. "I had a hard time... I thought if I could just make enough money, then it would all be okay. I just had to work. I was sure I'd figure everything out."

More tears. The woman leaked more than bad plumbing. And everything in him wanted to fix it for her. Because beyond the beauty, beyond the walls she'd put up, lay a woman he was drawn to. A woman he wanted to know. A woman in pain.

She wiped her eyes. "I got a job dancing again."

Why didn't that sound like good news?

She raised her hand, made air quotes. "Dancing."

It took him a second. Then he realized what she meant.

"It wasn't a... Vegas is..." She swallowed. "I always wore something. It was barely anything, but—"

"You don't have to—"

"I'm just saying."

"Okay."

She was quiet a moment while he tried very hard not to picture what she'd described. Tried very hard to push away the anger, the disgust. Not at her, but at every person who'd seen her, every person who'd taken advantage of her desperation.

Finally, she continued. "You start doing that for a living, and the last thing you want is to have a *better* grip on reality. I used more drugs, drank more, partied more. Anything to forget."

He couldn't imagine. Didn't want to.

"I met a guy. He was... I didn't realize how much he was like the first guy. I mean, not in all the ways you can see. The first guy was rich, this one was poor. The first guy was classy and sophisticated, this one was down to earth and funny. But they were alike in the ways that mattered. I chose not to see it, because I so desperately needed somebody to... to love me, I guess."

He kept his mouth shut. On his lap, his hands were clenched so tightly they hurt.

"Money was always an issue," she said. "I made it, he spent it. Then..." Her gaze started darting again. Here, there. Anywhere but at him. "He got arrested. Sent to prison."

He hadn't expected that. "What did you do?"

There was a long pause. "This and that. And then I ended up with Gramps."

This and that. What did that mean? Not that it was any of his business. She hadn't had to tell him all of that. She hadn't had to tell him any of it. So why had she? And why had she stopped?

And what did *this and that* mean?

"You still haven't gone home?"

"How can I, after...?"

He thought of his own parents. The love they'd always shown him. He knew all parents weren't like his, though. "Are you afraid they'll reject you?"

"Wouldn't you?"

He unclenched his fists and rested his hand on hers. Tried to ignore the electricity that zinged through him. "No. I wouldn't."

She met his gaze, blinked, looked down.

"What if they didn't reject you, Harper?" At the sound of her name, she met his eyes. "What if they greeted you with open arms? What if they hugged you and held you and told you how much they loved you?"

More tears. "What if they didn't?"

"What would you have lost?"

When she didn't answer, he pulled his hand back. At least now he understood the haunted look in her eyes, the reason she chose to be alone rather than with family.

But there were those bruises. And there was Red.

"Did your grandfather have a falling out with them, too?"

She blinked. Twice. "Uh. He hasn't had a relationship with them in a long time."

"Why not?"

She shrugged and carried her plate to the trash, where she dumped what she hadn't eaten. "I don't know the story. Don't ask him about it, though. He doesn't like to talk about it."

Amazing how fast the woman could shift from truth to lies. After all she'd told him, what in the world could she be hiding?

CHAPTER EIGHTEEN

Derrick stepped out of the shower in his Las Vegas hotel room Tuesday morning and dripped on the fancy tile while he dried off. This had been an utterly useless trip. He'd been so sure he'd be able to locate Harper. Where else would she go except back to the crappy life she'd left?

All day Friday and then all weekend, he'd looked for her. But nobody at the nursing home where she'd been working had seen her since she'd moved away. He'd even offered money for information on her whereabouts. Zip, zero, nada.

Derrick had visited her old apartment building and canvassed the residents, but they all claimed not to remember her. Those people were probably lucky to remember their names half the time. Bunch of bums. Even those fools at the grocery store where Harper had worked for chump change had come up with squat. Trying to grease their palms had gotten him nothing.

Unfortunately, it was Vegas, and without Harper to distract him, the poker tables had beckoned.

When he'd first met Harper, he'd believed she would be his angel. Once he'd turned his focus to her, his desire to gamble had waned. It had gone from a pounding need to a dull ache easily ignored. But when she'd blown him off over the summer because

Gramps was sick, that ache had grown, and, with nothing else to do, he'd gone to Atlantic City.

The money he'd lost—her fault. All her fault.

And he was back here in Vegas because of her. He'd lost more money because of her.

So now he was tapped out, and not just financially. He'd been winning all night. At one point, he'd had thousands of dollars' worth of chips stacked in front of him. He'd been so sure this would be the moment of his big score. The solution to all his problems. But by the time the sun rose over the distant mountains, he'd lost every penny.

Derrick scoffed at his reflection in the foggy mirror. His angel. Right. Thanks to Harper, he was pretty sure he'd soon get a visit from the angel of death.

Why couldn't she have just been on his side?

Didn't she understand what he'd done for her? Rescuing her from the low-class life she'd lived here, when she'd had to work two jobs just to get by. Derrick had given her a place to live and a job— a job nobody else would hire an ex-con to do. He'd showered her with gifts, given her everything she needed. He'd loved her.

And she'd betrayed him.

He dressed in a fresh suit and tie and checked his image in the mirror, smiling at his reflection despite the fury filling his gut. He still looked like the kind of guy you could trust with your money. And people could trust him. At least he'd kept that part of his life unsullied.

He slipped on his glasses, packed his small roller bag, and headed for the elevator.

He'd never be back. Never. Not to Las Vegas, not to Atlantic City, not to any of the other casinos that had popped up all over the country like zits on a teenager. After last night, he was done with gambling forever.

He meant it this time.

Thank God he'd put most of the cash he'd gotten from Tank into his savings account, an account not accessible by ATM and not attached to his checking account. No matter how much he'd wanted to dig into it the night before, he hadn't been able to. So he'd only lost the money he'd had on him.

Only. Like a thousand dollars was chump change.

Except it was, compared to what he owed. And now he had less cash to use for finding Harper and Gramps.

As he pushed the button to summon the elevator, he cursed the cards that had turned against him, his own stupidity, and Harper.

Someone approached from behind.

A man stood to his right, another behind him. Too close. He turned to nod, felt his automatic smile freeze.

He didn't recognize them, but he didn't need to. Their sneers told Derrick all he needed to know. He faced them head-on. The shorter one snatched Derrick's suitcase. The one shaped like Rambo gripped Derrick's arm as if he were in the mood for juice and Derrick was the orange.

"Let's take a walk," Rambo said.

Fighting would only get him hurt. Yelling for help would prob-ably get him knocked out cold. He walked with the men to the room next door to the one he'd occupied. How long had they been watching?

They knocked, and a man on the inside opened the door.

This one, Derrick recognized. Quentin Gray. Medium height, medium build, medium red hair, medium brown eyes. Freckles all over his face. Didn't look a day over twenty-five, but Derrick guessed he was at least in his thirties. He passed himself off as a tech millionaire, and maybe he was. He'd developed some obscure program for some obscure industry. But that program didn't account for the bulk of his income. That came from other, more lucrative, sources.

One of which was the reason Derrick was face-to-face with him now.

The goons pushed Derrick into the room and followed. The door closed with a thud.

Quentin crossed to a small desk and sat in the chair behind it.

"You've been avoiding me."

Derrick shrugged off Rambo and forced himself not to rub his aching arm. He straightened his suit coat, pushed up his glasses, and stepped closer to Quentin, mostly to distance himself from the guys behind him. "I didn't know you were in Las Vegas."

"When I heard you were in town, I thought I'd fly in, say hello."

Derrick was smart enough not to ask how he'd heard. "I'm trying to get your money."

Quentin took his phone, pressed the screen, then lifted it so Derrick could see the image there.

Photos of him at the poker table the night before. The first photo showed a stack of chips in front of him. He wore a stupid smile. Quentin swiped so Derrick could look at the next photo. Fewer chips, smaller smile. Then he saw the next, and the next, until finally, no chips remained in front of him. Derrick stared at the image of his own face, the shock he saw there, as if any idiot couldn't have seen that coming. As if the same thing hadn't happened every single time.

Derrick looked past the phone to the man. "I'm back on the wagon today."

"Figured you'd turn your paltry cash into the two hundred grand you owe me?"

Derrick tried his most charming smile. "Worth a try."

Quentin pocketed his phone and shook his head slowly. "I don't know what we're going to do with you. We tried talking sense into you—"

"I've got a—"

"I was sure," Quentin said, "after we had that little chat with your girlfriend, you'd come to your senses."

Derrick tried to blink away the images that reminder brought. Harper, black-and-blue and terrified after the attack. She'd known it was his fault. What she hadn't grasped was that it was her fault, too. If she'd worked with him instead of against him, he'd have gotten the money from Gramps months ago.

"I'm doing everything I can," Derrick said. "And that little stunt of yours just made it harder."

"Stunt, huh?" Quentin looked beyond Derrick to the goons behind him. "Can you believe this guy?"

Rambo and his sidekick remained silent.

Derrick pushed his glasses up. "Look, I've got a plan. I'll get your money, every penny."

Quentin's gaze was hard. "Money isn't the only issue."

"What does that mean?"

"My guys in Baltimore, they're missing. You know anything about that?"

Derrick's mind raced. Guys in Baltimore? Who could he...? "You mean Keith and his goon friend?"

Behind him, Rambo grunted. Maybe *goon* hadn't been the best word choice.

"I had two men on the payroll, and you were one of their jobs. They reported their chit-chat with your girlfriend, and I haven't heard from them since."

Rambo approached from behind. Derrick didn't turn, but he could feel the man's heat on his back, his breath on his neck.

"My employees get nervous when fellow employees go missing."

"I don't know anything about that," Derrick said.

Rambo dropped a huge hand on Derrick's shoulder, squeezed the trapezius muscle hard.

Derrick was on his knees almost before the pain registered. "I swear, I know nothing." His voice was high-pitched, but he couldn't lower it. "Harper and my grandfather disappeared that weekend. Maybe she did something to them."

Behind him, the goon removed his hand, and Derrick had to fight to keep from collapsing in a heap. He rubbed the sore spot, swallowed hard, and stood.

"If we learn you came against my men"—Quentin's words were slow and measured and deadly serious—"you'll want to do yourself in before one of us gets to you."

He lifted his hands, palms out. "I have no idea what happened. I never saw them that weekend."

Quentin nodded and tapped the table in front of him with a pen. "If you can't come up with the cash, I can think of some other ways to get what's owed me. I have an associate who might be interested in a trade, and that girlfriend of yours... I've done a little digging. Seems she might be able to earn back—"

"I'll get you the money." At this point, Harper didn't deserve better than what Quentin was suggesting, but Derrick couldn't stomach any other man's hands on her. She was his. Until he was done with her, she belonged to him.

Quentin dropped the pen on the desk and stood. "I've given you extension after extension, listened to your promises over and over. No more lies, no more promises. And there'll be no payment plans. I expect the entire balance in one week."

A week? Even if he found Gramps and did him in, he wouldn't get his inheritance in a week. "That's not enough time." He'd tried to keep his voice measured but failed, and the words had come out squeaky and scared.

A smile spread across Quentin's features. "Between your wealthy grandfather and your, shall we say, talented girlfriend, I'm sort of hoping you don't make your deadline. Seems I might be able to find a way to get back my investment with interest. And I won't need you at all. Of course, once I no longer need you..." He shrugged. "Nobody gets away with not paying me back."

Derrick swallowed a huge lump in his throat.

Quentin laughed, looked past Derrick. "You should see his face. White as a corpse."

That elicited a chuckle from one of the goons.

Derrick tried to act nonchalant, act as if he received death threats all the time. He glanced at his watch. "I have a flight."

Quentin stood, gestured toward the door. "Don't let us keep you."

Derrick started to turn, but Quentin held him in place with a lifted palm. He looked past Derrick again. "Doesn't seem fair that his girlfriend got beat up and he walked away without a scrape."

Behind him, one of them gripped his upper arms.

"We don't want to do anything that'll keep him from paying me back." He gave Derrick a quick assessment. "He seems a bit delicate."

Derrick's arms ached from the man's meaty grip, but he tried to look tough and unconcerned.

Quentin said, "Just pop one of his eyes out and send him on his way."

Before he could react, the goon flipped him off his feet. Derrick landed on his back, lost his breath.

Rambo straddled him and pressed his arms into the floor.

The smaller goon leaned over Derrick's head. He used one hand to hold his eye open. In the other, Derrick saw the glint of a knife.

It closed in.

He had no breath to scream. No energy to fight. All he could do was lie there and watch as the knife neared his face. The little goon smiled.

An eternity passed before Quentin laughed. "All right, all right. Let him keep the eye for now."

The goons let him go and stood, relaxed, as if this were the most normal situation in the world.

The whole thing had happened so fast, Derrick still didn't have his breath back.

Then, Rambo kicked him in the side.

Derrick rolled in to the fetal position and waited for more blows.

"Look at me," Quentin said.

Derrick forced himself to shift, though his ribs protested the movement. He sat up and did as he was told.

Quentin's lips pressed together as he shook his head. "I don't know why I keep giving you chances to betray me. But hey, I guess I'm just a good guy. Trusting, you know? So here you are. One.

Last. Chance. You blow it, you're dead, and I'll get what I need from your grandfather and that girlfriend of yours."

Derrick struggled to stand, tried to get air into his lungs.

The sidekick opened the door and looked up and down the hall. Then Rambo pushed Derrick out of the room. He stumbled and crashed against the opposite door and fell in a heap.

One of them tossed his suitcase on top of him. The door slammed, leaving Derrick alone.

He couldn't move, couldn't think.

Finally he got a deep breath, touched his eyes to reassure himself they were both there. His ribs throbbed. Broken, bruised? Should he go to the emergency room?

He didn't know. Couldn't think.

His shoulder ached.

He pressed a hand to his head where it had hit the door. A knot was already forming.

Slowly, muscles protesting and lungs tight, he used the door knob to pull himself up and hobbled to the elevator, dragging his suitcase behind him.

Every minute waiting for the elevator was torture. He needed to be around people, somewhere Quentin and his goons couldn't hurt him again. He'd take the stairs but feared he might pass out.

Finally, the elevator came, and he stepped in beside a mother with two kids. She took one look at him and pulled her kids behind her.

In the lobby, Derrick made his way toward the front door to get a taxi to the airport. Those few minutes in Quentin's hotel room had been terrifying, but they could have ended so much worse.

Derrick was walking away.

He would get Quentin's money. He just had to get his hands on Gramps and Harper and figure out a way to get Gramps to hand over two hundred grand. If Derrick had to hurt them... Well, the old man shouldn't have been so stingy.

And Harper shouldn't have betrayed him.

They both had it coming.

CHAPTER NINETEEN

Tuesday turned out to be a beautiful day. The sky was bright blue, and the temperature was predicted to hit a very unseasonable sixty-five. Jack had worked double-time to finish the projects he'd started the day before. He caught up by lunchtime and was on his way to look at a multi-unit property in the next town when Ginny called to reschedule.

"Let's do it tomorrow," she said. "Meanwhile, you keep visualizing the kind of property you want to find."

He rolled his eyes and swallowed his retort. "I'll pray about it, too."

"Right," she said. "Well, then…"

They made an appointment for the following day, and he turned the truck around too fast, causing it to slide on the gravely road. He'd really been looking forward to seeing the place. He should go home, get some painting done. Except the weather was so beautiful.

And he couldn't stop thinking about Red and Harper, his confusion and her bruises. They'd faded now, but after Red's aggression the day before…

He was traveling through downtown Nutfield when he turned

on a whim and parked at the food bank. He let himself in the back door.

It wasn't a client day, so the warehouse was empty of people. Voices came from the rec center, but he passed the entrance and knocked on the door to Vanessa's office.

On the other side of the door, he heard the scrape of a chair, then Vanessa's voice. "Come in."

He opened the door to find a man standing in front of her desk. Her eyebrows were lifted. "We are finished here."

"Look," the man said, "I'm just trying to—"

"I have it under control." Vanessa regarded him with a cool look. "But I thank you for your concern."

"For your clients," the man said.

In the awkward silence that followed, Jack said, "I'm sorry, I didn't mean..."

The man turned. He was a little taller than Jack, maybe a little older, and right now, his jaw was clenched tight. "Not your fault. The woman's stubborn streak is wider than the Atlantic."

He brushed past Jack, who turned to Vanessa with raised eyebrows. "You okay?"

She waved off his comment and the man who'd just stormed off. "He had some ideas, which I said I would think about. He calls me stubborn. He has all the patience of a newborn with a ... a bottom rash."

"Diaper rash?"

She waved that off, too. "What do you need?"

He nodded toward the chair across from her desk. "Do you mind?"

"One moment." She tapped on her keyboard before she pushed it away and turned to him.

Jack sat. "I wanted to talk to you about Harper and Red."

"Harper apologized. Apparently her phone does not work well."

"So she said."

"She told me to call McNeal's if something else happens, and I said I would do that."

"Yeah, I figured."

"You know everything. Why are you here?"

He tried to stop the smile but failed. Some people found her abrasive, but he knew better. Vanessa had built a wall around herself, this facade of anger. But he'd known her long enough to see the big heart underneath.

Maybe whatever had caused her to build her wall had enabled her to see beyond Harper's. "I'm worried about them. When they first moved in, Harper had some bruises."

"I saw the one on her cheek," she said. "There were others?"

"A big one on her arm. And maybe a sprained wrist. Seemed like she was favoring it. I was just wondering if you think... I don't know what to do. Red's such a nice guy, but you saw him yesterday. I wonder if, when he has those episodes—"

"You think he did that to her?"

"Not on purpose. I don't know what to think."

Vanessa looked past him, her bottom lip caught between her teeth. Finally, she said, "I do not think so. I think she is here because of those bruises, no?"

"Oh." That made sense. "You're saying she came to Nutfield—"

"Because some man showed his displeasure with his fists. Do you not think so?"

"I hadn't—"

"And if her grandfather had given her those bruises, then why would she have brought the problem with her?"

"That's a good point. But..." He told her about the cut to Harper's forehead.

"What did she say about it?"

"That he didn't mean to do it."

"Then you must believe her. If she wants to confide in you, she will. But do not be surprised if she doesn't. Women in her situation do not trust men easily."

The image of the man who'd just stormed out flashed in Jack's mind. Vanessa didn't trust men so easily, either. Jack knew that well enough. She'd treated him just as coolly when he'd first started volunteering. He wasn't sure she trusted him now.

Jack stood. "Thanks for your advice. If she tells you anything you feel like I need to know…"

Her eyebrows rose.

"I mean, as her landlord and neighbor, I want to make sure she's safe."

"We will have to trust Harper to share what she wants to share with whom she wants to share it."

Jack walked out of Vanessa's office feeling not at all reassured. How could he keep Harper safe if he had no idea who he was trying to protect her from?

He decided not to examine why he felt it was his responsibility.

It wouldn't hurt to check on Red, make sure everything was okay after the episode the day before. Maybe Red would be lucid enough to tell him about his real estate business. And maybe he'd give Jack some insight about what was going on with them.

He stepped into the rec center. A couple of women were sitting on the couches facing the TV. Red and Steve, as usual, were seated at the game table with playing cards spread in front of them.

Red pushed himself to his feet when Jack walked in. "Good to see you, son. It's been a while. Where you been?"

Jack gripped his outstretched hand and glanced at Steve, who was shaking his head slightly. Seemed Red had no memory of the day before.

"Keeping busy," Jack said. "How about you?"

He lowered himself into the chair. "Just beating Steve at gin."

"You wish, old man." Steve's oversize ears wiggled with his smile.

Jack sat between them. "Don't let me stop you."

The men resumed their game, and Jack watched for a few minutes. They both seemed sharp and aware.

"I was hoping you'd tell me about your real estate business, Red," Jack said.

Red picked up a card, studied it, and set it on the discard pile. "What do you wanna know?"

Jack shrugged. "Whatever you want to tell me, I guess. I'm trying to learn all I can."

For the next hour, Red and Steve regaled Jack with stories of their real estate ventures. It didn't take long for the men to start one-upping each other, though it was clear that while Steve had only dabbled, Red had built a solid enterprise.

"At one point," Red said, "I owned over five hundred rental units. Most of them were small apartment buildings or multifamily homes."

"Lot of work," Jack said.

"Sure, sure. But it wasn't like I managed them."

Jack was the manager for a lot of local investors, so he understood the importance of that part of the business. He hoped to be able to farm out the management of his properties one day, too.

"But you sold most of them?" Jack asked.

Red picked up the deck of cards, which by then had been sitting, forgotten, on the table for some time. He shuffled it a few times.

Something in the man's eyes kept both Jack and Steve quiet. Was that regret? For what?

Finally, Red tapped the edge of the cards on the table and set the deck down. "I sold almost all of them, put the money in a trust for my grandson." He blinked. "Grandkids, I mean."

Jack didn't miss the slip. What did it mean? "Why'd you get out?"

"Too much work for an old man. Got to where I'd look at the numbers, and I just couldn't... They didn't make sense to me like they used to."

Jack wrestled with something to say. He ended up with, "Well, that sucks."

Red chuckled. "Gettin' old ain't for sissies, kid, lemme tell you."

"You said it." Steve slammed his hand on the table.

The white-haired woman looked up from her needlepoint and shushed them.

Red and Steve chuckled. "The librarian's mad at us," Red whispered.

Jack's question must've shown on his face, because Steve tipped his head toward the women. "Forty years she worked as a school librarian. Never seen her with a book, but lemme tell you, she doesn't put up with loud pupils."

Jack chuckled, focused on Red again. "The other day, you said you still owned some properties."

"I haven't been able to part with my earliest investments. They're single-family homes, and they got me started. Helped me believe I could do it. They have sentimental value. And the renters have been there forever. When the renters move out, I'll sell."

Jack pulled out his cell and navigated to the link his Realtor had sent him. "I'm thinking about buying this place." He showed Red the property.

The old man peered through his glasses with narrowed eyes. "How much per unit."

Jack told him, then went on to explain what he knew about the place. "Most of the units have been updated, and the plumbing is—"

"All that stuff'll break," Red said. "Figure everything in the house will eventually need to be replaced or repaired over the life of the loan."

Jack nodded slowly while the man's words penetrated. "I'd never thought of it that way."

"If you're in this for the long haul, you have to. That's how people screw this up. They look at income and expenses, but they forget that, over thirty years, there'll be a lot of repairs. So you have to plan on that, put away money to cover new furnaces and roofs and water heaters, and—"

"Floors and paint and appliances," Steve said. "And everybody wants air conditioning now. In my day, we could handle a little heat, but nowadays people think it's inhumane if every room isn't kept at seventy degrees."

Their suggestions spun in Jack's mind. What the men were saying made sense. But that would definitely affect his numbers. "Looks like I've got some work to do."

Red squeezed his shoulder. "You'll get there."

An idea crossed his mind. "Hey, do you want to go for a ride with me, drive by the place? It's only about fifteen minutes away."

"I been staring at Steve's ears long enough. I'd love to."

Jack turned to Steve. "How about you? Would you be able—?"

"Elizabeth's picking me up. I'll wait for her."

Jack started to stand, then glanced at his watch and sat back down. "Actually, I probably need to check with Harper, make sure she doesn't mind."

Red waved him off. "Use that phone you got there and give her a ring. She won't care."

Jack stepped out of the rec center and was dialing when Harper walked in the back door. She froze when she saw him. Was that a blush that rose to her cheeks?

He hoped not. He certainly hoped she wasn't embarrassed about all she'd told him the day before. His problem wasn't what she *had* told him but what she *hadn't*. And he knew there had been plenty left unsaid.

He took a few steps toward her. "I was just about to call you."

She approached as if he were a hostile animal. "It was slow, so Bonnie let me go early." She stopped a few feet from him. "Is Gramps okay?"

He hoped his smile would relax her. "He's fine. I was going to ask if you'd mind if I took him for a ride. Now that you're here, you can join us."

"A ride where?"

"I'm looking at a property, and I thought your grandfather might be able to give me some advice."

Her eyes narrowed. "He's not strong enough to be traipsing all over—"

"We were just going to drive by. It's a nice day. I figured he might like to get out in the sunshine."

She bit her bottom lip. Her gaze flicked to the door to the rec center. "He wants to go with you?"

"Said he did."

She swallowed. "I guess that's okay."

"Good," Jack said. "You can leave your car here and go with us. I'll drive."

"I'll go on home. You two don't need me."

That was true. They didn't. But now that she was here, he craved her company. "I thought we'd look at the house, then maybe drive over to the beach and get some ice cream."

Her lips twitched. "It's not *that* warm outside."

"In New Hampshire, sunshine means ice cream. The temperature is irrelevant."

He could practically see her gears moving, trying to decide what to do.

"It's really good ice cream," he added.

Finally, she smiled for real. "You talked me into it."

CHAPTER TWENTY

Harper watched the world slide by from the backseat of Jack's pickup. The evergreens shone greener against the backdrop of the sapphire blue sky. The forest on either side of the road called to her, deep and inviting. This land of trees and trees and more trees was so different from where she'd grown up in Kansas. When she was a kid, she'd loved those wide-open spaces, the skies that burst in color every morning and night. There was a little rise not far from her house in Wichita where she used to ride her bike. From the very crest, she'd have sworn she could see all the way to Canada. She used to imagine some little girl looking south toward her, wearing a heavy jacket and a knit cap and waving. The years since had taught Harper her vision wasn't nearly as good as she'd once believed.

Nowadays, she could barely see her next step.

What had Gramps told her? God's word was a lamp unto her feet? She wished it were more like a street lamp and less like a cheap flashlight with a dying bulb.

When she'd been young, all those open spaces had made her feel very small in the universe. Small, but she'd always known she was loved. Now, as Harper peered at the tops of trees that made the ones back home look like oversize bushes, she felt that small-ness again. Small, insignificant, and lost.

Up front, Jack and Gramps talked real estate. She couldn't keep up with their conversation and didn't care to. All she could think about—all she'd thought about since Jack had left her house the previous day—were the confessions she'd made to him.

As if he were her priest, not her landlord.

She needed more than a drive in the country and some ice cream. She needed a brain transplant.

Seriously. Had Jack needed to know all her ugly history? Now that he knew, he could never un-know. To him, she'd forever be a former exotic dancer.

Fine, then. Who cared what he thought? As long as he didn't assume she'd give him a private show, they were fine. Maybe now he'd stop asking her questions, stop trying to dig into her life.

She swiped her stupid tears. Her heart didn't understand what her head knew. That, as desperately as she wanted a friend, she couldn't have one. Eventually, everyone would ask questions she couldn't answer, questions that would only get her in trouble. She and Gramps couldn't run again. Gramps wouldn't survive. And the only way to stay here was to fly under the radar.

Keep her head down and her mouth shut.

So what in the world was she doing in the backseat of Jack Rossi's pickup truck?

Definitely time for that brain transplant.

But Gramps was with them. She was safe from spitting out all her secrets as long as she didn't end up alone with Jack. That was when her mind got muddled and confused.

The truck slowed, and Jack turned into a parking lot that served three white buildings.

"All of them?" Gramps asked.

Jack nodded and peered through the windshield at the two-story structures. The buildings were square and so close together they were practically joined at the corners like spaces on a checker-board. The parking lot sat in front of them. Jack was thinking of buying this? What must it be like to have that kind of freedom, that kind of optimism?

"Each one has eight apartments," Jack said. "Four downstairs, four up."

Gramps was nodding slowly. "Twenty-four apartments, but only three roofs. Only one parking lot to maintain. Only a handful of walkways that need to be cleared of snow and ice. Something to be said for that."

Jack focused on him. "Am I crazy to take on such a huge project? All I have under my belt is your house and mine."

"And years of management experience," Gramps said.

Harper studied the old man as he focused on the buildings. His mind seemed to be churning, considering. She loved watching him work. She'd seen so little of that since Derrick had tried to con him out of money this summer. Between his worsening dementia, the viruses he'd battled, and the antifreeze—not to mention his broken heart after what Derrick had done—it had been a long time since Gramps had been interested in anything but the TV. Today, he seemed one hundred percent the real estate investor he'd been for thirty years.

Gramps turned to Jack. "You need to pull together those numbers we talked about. Bring them by when you're ready, and we'll talk through it."

Jack took one last look at the building. "I'll do that. I can't tell you how much I appreciate your help."

"Glad somebody values me. That idiot grandkid of mine..."

Harper patted Gramps's shoulder.

He glanced at her, mouth pinched shut.

After a pause, Jack shifted into drive. "Let's go get that ice cream."

Gramps wasn't in the habit of talking about Derrick with strangers, mostly because there was very little good he could say. But he was coming to trust Jack. As long as he didn't let the truth slip, they should be all right.

But what if he did? She'd need a story, a plausible story to explain her dishonesty. And she'd need to improve her skills at lying.

Please, God. Tell me how to handle this.

There was no answer. She envied those people who seemed so close to God, they heard His voice. Right now, there was nothing she could do but stay on this ride and hope it would come to a soft landing.

Jack weaved through some of the prettiest little villages Harper had ever seen. Bright white churches and lovely town commons with gleaming monuments and colorful parks. They passed old farmhouses, some just a few feet from the road, with pretty barns and lush bushes and towering trees. Finally, they turned a corner and crested a hill, and she got her first glimpse of the rocky New England coast.

"Wow." Her word was barely a whisper.

Jack glanced at her in the rearview mirror. "I thought you'd like it."

"It's breathtaking."

They turned onto the road that hugged the shoreline. She was mesmerized by the waves as they crashed against the boulders below. On the other side of the street, mansions of every shape and style overlooked the raging waters. Many had platforms standing above the roofs.

"I bet those are good for sunbathing," she said.

Jack glanced at one particularly huge house. "Those are widows' walks."

"Back in the day," Gramps said, "women would watch for ships, waiting for their husbands and sons and fathers to return."

She could imagine it, the women's fears, the prayers they'd lift up from their perches above the sea, prayers for a glimpse of the ships that would bring their loved ones home. Harper's perch was her floor and her knees, and her prayers were for a glimpse of freedom from this crazy situation she'd found herself in. A hope for a future.

They stopped at a little white building with a sign shaped like an ice cream cone. A few folks were sitting at the outdoor picnic benches enjoying their treats.

Jack parked and opened her door.

She slid out. "Thanks."

He grabbed Gramps's walker from the bed of his pickup and hurried to help him out.

A cold breeze blew in from the ocean, and she shivered. Slowly, they walked toward the window on the side of the building.

"What's your poison?" Jack said.

"Hot chocolate?" she suggested.

He chuckled and shifted them toward a door. "We can eat inside."

They stepped into the tiny—and blessedly heated—dining room. Two of the six tables were occupied, one with an older couple, the other with two teenage girls. The girls seemed to be focused more on the long-haired boy behind the counter than on their cones.

Harper studied the board and settled on strawberry.

Jack shook his head as if he'd never been more disappointed. "I pegged you for a mint chocolate chip girl."

"So far off, you're not even on the radar."

Jack turned to Gramps. "How about you?"

"Cookies-and-cream for me," he said.

"Good choice." Jack placed their order. When Harper reached for her wallet, he stopped her with a hand on her arm. "My treat."

She considered arguing, then decided against it. She couldn't afford it, and Jack knew that.

This place was shifting her mood. Yes, her life was falling apart. Yes, she was tangled in a web of deception she might never escape. But the ocean, the blue skies, this charming ice cream parlor... There was something to be said for not being at work or at home, taking a break from the worries that weighed her down.

Jack handed her the ice cream cone, gave Gramps his double scoop of cookies-and-cream, and then sat with his own.

"What'd you get?" she asked.

"Peanut butter chocolate chip."

She regarded his cone. "Looks yummy."

He leaned it toward her. "Try it."

"Oh, well..."

"Go on," he said. "It won't kill you."

She licked a tiny spot, and he scoffed. "You can do better than that."

She took a bigger bite, tasted the salty peanut butter and sweet chocolate. "You're right. That's good."

"Now you'll know for next time."

Next time.

Wouldn't that be nice?

Gramps settled against the wall and stared out the window and across the street at the long stone jetty that reached into the ocean. "Sure is pretty here."

"Is it much different from the coastline where you're from?" Jack's question was aimed at her.

"Uh..." She'd only seen Rehoboth Beach in Delaware. "It's rockier." She turned to Red. "What do you think?"

He shrugged. "Much colder."

Jack chuckled, gaze on Harper again. "I've only ever been to beaches in New England."

Harper swallowed a bite of ice cream. She didn't have much information to compare. But if she were Gramps's granddaughter... "We didn't go to the beach a lot."

"We didn't go to the beach a lot when I was a kid, either," Jack said. "Our vacations were usually in the mountains."

She focused on her ice cream, had to keep quiet. Keep all her secrets. If she started talking, they'd slip out.

Gramps wiped a dribble of ice cream off his chin. "What did you do in the mountains?"

"In the winter," Jack said, "we skied. You guys ski?"

Harper said, "No," at the same time Gramps said, "Used to."

Jack looked between them again, focused on Harper. "You

should give it a try. I love it. What kinds of vacations did you go on?"

She thought of their summers spent in Eureka Springs, Arkansas. "We used to camp near a lake. We'd go swimming and boating. Sometimes, my parents rented jet skis." She loved the speed, the feel of the spray on her skin, the feeling of weightlessness when she got thrown off. Nutfield reminded her of that little lake town.

"I bet you're a boss on a jet ski," Jack said.

She nodded. "Pretty much."

He smiled and turned back to Gramps. "In the summer, we'd rent a place on a lake. My sisters and my mom would sleep in, shop, swim, and work on their tans."

"You?" Gramps asked.

"Dad and I would go hunting," Jack said.

"Hunting." Gramps grunted. "Never could stand it, sitting there in the freezing cold, staring at empty woods."

"I was up for doing whatever Dad wanted. And hunting was the only time he relaxed."

Gramps said, "Good guy, your dad?"

"The best." Jack worked on his cone, then glanced at her.

"So," she said to steer him away from questions about her past. "Besides hunting, what else did you and your dad do together?"

Jack's chuckle seemed filled with memories. "My dad worked a lot. He was the kind of guy who could never keep still."

"Kind of like you?" She'd observed that same boundless energy in Jack.

"Huh." Jack's gaze went to the ceiling before it settled on her. "You think?"

"Based on what I know of you."

He nodded slowly, seemed to be letting the idea settle. "Nobody I'd rather be compared to than my dad." He licked his ice cream.

She said, "You were about to tell us—"

"Right. So he worked a lot. We didn't see him much during the week. On the weekends, he was always doing something. The house we lived in was old, and Dad was forever fixing it up. Refinishing the hardwood, replacing tile, repairing plumbing. He could do everything. Install new light fixtures, build furniture, hang drywall. When I was in middle school, he built an addition to the house."

"Guy like that," Gramps said, "worth his weight in gold."

Jack aimed what was left of his ice cream cone toward Gramps. "You said it. And not just because he's handy. He wasn't a Christian back then, but he raised us right. When he did become a Christian, most of the family went right along with him."

A frown crossed his face like a shifting shadow, gone almost before she'd seen it. She suspected it had something to do with that remark—*most* of the family. Jack recovered before she could ask. "Anyway," he said, "I used to follow Dad around, and he'd teach me what he was doing. Sometimes, it would be so boring sitting there watching him work, but I loved being with him. And sometimes, Dad would realize how bored I was and stop for no reason except just because, and he'd take me for ice cream."

"Good memories," Gramps said.

Harper thought of her own father, of the times they'd spent together. She hadn't appreciated him when she was a kid. He was a good man, but she'd been too busy with her friends and social life and dreams to value her own father. Maybe if she'd shadowed him, everything would have been different.

They finished their ice cream. Gramps set down his dirty napkin and nodded toward the jetty. "Folks walking on that."

"You want to go?" Jack asked.

Harper gave him a look intended to say, *With his walker? Are you nuts?*

But Gramps only chuckled. "I wouldn't make it up the first steps. But you two should go."

Harper said, "I'm okay."

"We wouldn't want to abandon you," Jack added.

Gramps looked back and forth between them, his sharp eyes

missing nothing. "You two think I'm too old, too feeble, to sit here by myself a few minutes?"

"Of course not," Harper said.

Jack focused on her. "He's trying to goad us into taking a walk."

Gramps glared at her. "I promise I won't wander off or break a hip while you're gone."

She gathered the trash from the table. "I'm really not comfortable—"

"Ten minutes alone, girl," Gramps said. "Ten minutes to stare out at the sea and remember my Bebe. She'd have loved it here." He inhaled a long breath, shook his head, and blew it out. "Is that too much to ask?"

She looked to Jack for help. He gently took the trash she was squeezing in her fist, dropped it in the can, and held his hand out to her. "Come on. He'll be fine."

Defeated, she leaned down, kissed Gramps on the cheek. "You sure?"

He patted her arm. "I'll be right here when you get back."

Just what she needed—to be alone with Jack. His hand was still reaching toward her. What else could she do but slip hers into it. Together, they stepped into the sunny day.

CHAPTER TWENTY-ONE

Jack was having a hard time focusing. The day was beautiful, the sun was shining, the waves were crashing against the rocks across the street, but his mind was on the soft, chilled hand wrapped in his and the woman beside him.

They reached the edge of the road, and Harper looked behind them. "You sure he'll be okay?"

Jack looked, too. Folks were congregated at the tables around the ice cream parlor soaking up the sun. "How far can he go?"

"What if he gets sick or something?"

Jack squeezed her hand. "He wanted to be alone."

"I know." She sighed and turned toward the street. At a break in traffic, they darted to the far side.

He climbed the rocks of the jetty before helping her up. When she was steady, they turned toward the sea and walked. She kept her hand in his.

The rocks on top were mostly flat, but Jack and Harper still had to be careful not to slip.

The wind whipped Harper's hair, and she pushed it out of her face. He glimpsed the tiny cut on her forehead that she'd gotten a week earlier. It seemed to be healing well. Her bruises had faded completely.

He wanted to ask her about them, but Vanessa's words reverberated in his ears. She didn't trust him enough to tell him. Questioning her wouldn't make that better.

They made it to the end of the jetty, where she stared out at the blue waves, at the rocky coastline to the north dotted with little cabins and giant mansions and hotels and ice cream stands and restaurants. To the south lay Hampton Beach and the boardwalk with its tourist shops and arcades and hotels and rental cabins.

"It's so beautiful," she said.

He forced his gaze away from her face to see what she was seeing. "It is."

For a moment, she seemed as carefree as the seagulls cawing overhead.

She turned his direction and met his gaze. "I say this a lot."

"What's that?"

"Thank you." She gestured to the scene surrounding them. "I needed this today."

He shrugged. "Sure."

"You've been a good friend to us." She met his gaze, her blue eyes watery and sincere, her cheeks pink in the chilly wind, her hair blowing behind her like some sort of sea goddess. She seemed lost, alone in the world except for an old man who needed her. She was lonely, frightened, needy, and everything in him wanted to help. To give her everything she needed, everything he had.

"I'm sorry I'm so..." She looked back out to sea. "I should be a better friend. It's been a hard transition."

He stared at her silhouette and fought the urge to pull her to his chest, to hold her and tell her she could trust him. Waves of protectiveness and sheer desire washed over him. They lingered like salt after a dip in the ocean, seasoning his every thought. He swallowed, licked his lips. Touched her chin and urged her gaze back to his. Those eyes. He could dive into those eyes and stay forever.

They narrowed, and her head tilted to the side.

Right. She'd said something. He thought back, remembered. Something about the transition. "You're doing a wonderful job."

Her lips parted like she might speak, but she said nothing.

Hair blew across her face. He wanted to push it back, to feel the silky strands between his fingers.

She turned toward the shore and let go of his hand. "We should..."

No. He didn't want to go back. He liked the glimpse of the true Harper, the girl behind the mask. But the connection was broken. The memory of it wouldn't fade that quickly. If ever. "Okay."

They started back. He searched his brain for something to say, something innocuous, something that wouldn't push her away. Finally, what felt like a safe question entered his mind. "Where'd you grow up?"

She looked at him, eyes wide as if he'd just caught her stealing from the till.

Crap. Were there no fields that didn't contain land mines where this woman's past was concerned? "I figured it wasn't Maryland. I mean, since you don't ski and didn't have much to say about the coast. Maybe you visited as a kid. You and your grandfather have a good relationship." He was babbling. It seemed to be working as the shock in her expression faded.

They reached a gap in the rocks, and she focused on her steps. "Wichita, Kansas."

It sounded true. "I don't think I've ever met anybody from Kansas."

"Never been there?"

"Never been that far west. What's it like?"

"Flat. Skies as wide as..." She looked around, and her lips quirked in an almost smile. "As wide as this, actually. Except instead of ocean, we have grassland."

"And tornadoes?"

"I've never been swept away, so you can keep the Dorothy jokes to yourself."

"Dog named Toto?"

"Not even close." She walked a few steps and added, "Dog was named Lassie."

"All sorts of American film references going on."

She giggled. An actual joyful, troubles-abandoned, I-trust-you-at-least-for-this-second giggle. The sound made his heart race, his palms sweat in the cold breeze. That giggle did something to his insides, something he'd better not name. Something he'd better figure out how to undo and fast.

But she looked at him, those blue eyes sparkling like the water beneath him, and he knew there was no undoing it.

"Lassie was not named after Lassie."

He tried to make sense of that. "Okay."

"He was named after Bobbie Douglass, former KU quarterback. Played most of his NFL career for the Bears. How Douglass became Lassie, I have no idea."

It was Jack's turn to laugh. "I'm sure you'll be shocked to know that I've never heard of him."

She shrugged. "He's before our time."

"Is your mom a big KU fan?"

"Both my parents are."

"Huh." He tried to fit those pieces into the puzzle. "How'd your dad become such a KU fan if he's from Maryland?"

"Oh." She looked forward, swallowed.

Another landmine tripped.

"He went to college there," she said.

"That makes sense." And it would have, if she were a better liar.

Truth was, none of it made sense.

She switched from truth to lies so fast. But the fact that she was so bad at it told him something. Told him her entire life wasn't built on lies. For whatever reason, she felt she needed them right now. And that wasn't okay.

Yet, somehow, her lies didn't push him away. Because he'd known this woman just over a week. He'd seen her tender care for her grandfather. He'd watched her labor to provide for them both. Whatever was going on with her, he couldn't suspect her of wrongdoing.

And no matter how little he wanted to admit it, he was falling for her.

CHAPTER TWENTY-TWO

The next morning, at the start of her shift, Harper stared at the schedule posted in the kitchen at McNeal's.

The door behind her swished open, and she glanced at Bonnie as the woman beelined toward her.

Harper tapped her finger against her name scrawled beside the evening hours. "I have nobody to stay with Gramps."

The older woman took a deep breath. "I know you don't want to work evenings, but my grandson's in a recital, and I'm not gonna miss it. Nobody else can do it."

"*I* can't do it."

Bonnie crossed her arms. "You're doing a great job here, Harper. You fit right in, and the customers love you."

"Thank—"

"But I gotta have employees who can be flexible. If you can't, then maybe we need to rethink this."

The words settled in her gut like ice. She couldn't lose this job. She was barely getting by as it was.

Bonnie patted her on the shoulder. "You can take tomorrow off. I can get someone to—"

"No." She swallowed, shook her head. "No. I need all the

hours I can get." She focused again on the schedule. "Maybe I can bring Gramps with me."

"Ask Vanessa. I bet she'll know somebody who can keep an eye on him for you."

Harper turned, forced a smile. "Yeah. I'll do that. Thanks."

Vanessa probably would know somebody. Maybe one of Gramps's friends at the rec center would let him come hang out. Except evenings were his worst time. He did best when he was home, when he was in a familiar setting with familiar people. When he could fall in and out of sleep for a few hours in his chair before going straight to bed.

She had no idea what to do, but staring at the schedule wasn't going to help.

She tied her apron strings, grabbed her order pad, and headed into the dining room.

As she worked, the answer, the obvious answer, dogged her like a pesky fly.

Hadn't he already done enough for her?

How could she ask more of him?

As if conjured by her thoughts, the man in question arrived after the lunch crowd and was seated in one of her booths.

With a gaze at the ceiling, she thought, *Fine. I'll ask him.*

Jack saw her approaching and smiled as if she were the best thing he'd seen all day.

Wow. That smile.

How could she ask one more favor of this man? So far he hadn't acted as if he expected anything from her. But hadn't every man in her past fooled her?

"Hey," he said. "What's wrong?"

"Oh." She shook off her warring thoughts. "Sorry. Distracted. You know what you want?"

"I'll wait and order when Ginny gets here."

Ginny again. Right.

"I looked at those apartments this morning. I'm going to make an offer today."

"Oh. Good."

He shrugged. "I stopped by the rec center a little while ago, and your grandfather and I went over the numbers. I think it's a good deal, if I can get it for the right price."

"Then I hope you do."

His gaze held hers, and she couldn't seem to shake it off. He tilted his head to the side. "Is something wrong?"

"Oh, no. It's nothing." Her stomach churned as if she were standing up for an audition, not asking a neighbor for a favor. "I just... Bonnie had to schedule me for tonight, so I'm trying to figure out what to do with Gramps. I thought maybe—"

"No problem. What time?"

"I... Oh." The relief was so strong, she nearly had to sit down. "Thank you. I feel like I'm always needing something from you, and—"

"Sorry I'm late."

Harper turned as Jack's real estate agent slid into the seat across from him. She met Harper's eyes. "Haley, right?"

"Harper," Jack said.

"Oh. Sorry." She shook her head, smiled too widely. "I'm usually good at names." She closed her eyes, said, "Harper, like harpoon." The eyes popped open. "If I just visualize you harpooning a whale, I'll never forget again."

"Ahoy, matey," Harper said.

Ginny laughed. "It's a good trick. You should try it."

Harper closed her eyes, opened them, and said, "If I visualize you with a straw and a lime twist, I'll remember yours, too."

Ginny's smile faded just a bit. "Right. Well, then. I'll have a Sprite."

Harper turned to Jack, whose lips were fighting a smile. "Water for me."

Trying very hard not to look like Captain Ahab, Harper turned to fetch their drinks.

She kept an eye on them, delivering their lunches and refilling their drinks, as Jack and Ginny poured over paperwork spread across the table. They hardly spared her a glance when she asked if they needed anything else.

And if she caught Ginny looking at Jack with longing, at least she never saw the look returned.

Harper had cashed out all her customers but Jack by the time Ginny paid her bill and left. Harper approached the table. "Well?"

"She's going to fax the offer right now."

"Wow," she said. "This could really happen."

He pulled out his wallet, counted out some cash, and dropped the bills on the table. "I gotta run. What time tonight?"

"I need to be here at five."

"Aye-aye, captain." He winked. "I'll be over at four-thirty."

CHAPTER TWENTY-THREE

Derrick was parked a few houses down from Harper's childhood home in Wichita. He'd flown in from Vegas the day before, rented a car, and come straight here, and he'd been watching the house off and on ever since.

She had to be here.

Where else would she have gone? She'd always told him how much she wanted to reconcile with her family. She had little money and an old man to take care of. According to Roger, she hadn't used Gramp's debit card since the previous weekend. Seemed she and Gramps had been holed up in a hotel in Newark. But then she'd disappeared.

If she hadn't returned to Vegas, she must have come here.

But there'd been no sign of her. And except to use the bathroom and buy food, Derrick had hardly left this spot. He'd parked about a block down from her parents' house in the shade of an oak tree that kept dropping leaves and acorns on his rental.

He still couldn't get over the neighborhood. He knew she hadn't grown up poor, but still. The homes here were huge, and each sat on at least two acres of beautifully landscaped property. The house Harper had grown up in was one of the largest on the street, a two-story brick home with a three-car garage. The front porch was decorated with straw bales and potted mums. After the Thanksgiving holiday, he'd bet his last dollar those would be replaced with Christmas decorations.

How had a girl from this neighborhood ended up as a stripper in Vegas? Harper had told him the stories, but seeing her childhood home in person brought into perspective just how far she'd fallen.

Dreams of show business had lured her away.

Promises from lying men had kept her from coming home.

Derrick had never intended to be one of those lying men. He'd wanted to save Harper. Believed they could save each other. And they could have, if only she'd supported him.

There'd been a time when he'd hoped he and Harper could still make their relationship work. If she apologized, if she promised to be true to him... But with his arms, his back, and his pride all wounded after the showdown with Quentin, Derrick was well past caring a whit about Harper. He needed to find her because he needed Gramps's money. Gramps wouldn't turn over his money to Derrick voluntarily, but Harper could talk him into it. If she refused, then he'd use Gramps's love for her—love that should have been Derrick's—to get the cash.

It was still early in the day, but Derrick couldn't stand it any longer. He drove to the house, parked, and strode to the front steps. He'd seen her father leave for work an hour earlier, and he hadn't seen any sign of her brothers. According to Harper, the older was married, the younger college-aged. Her mother would be home alone.

Derrick knocked. A minute later, the door swung open.

The woman was a more mature version of Harper. Tall and slender with blond hair and blue eyes. "Can I help you?"

Derrick offered his most charming smile. "I hope so, ma'am. Are you Mrs. Cloud?"

"I am."

"My name is Derrick Burns. I'm a friend of your daughter."

The woman's eyes widened, and her jaw dropped a shade.

"Oh." She blinked twice. Then her eyes narrowed. "Has something happened?"

Derrick let his smile fade. "Not that I know of, but I'm worried about her safety." He let that hang in the air for a moment before he added, "Can I come in?"

The woman blinked, glanced beyond him, then behind her. "Are you with the police or something?"

"No, ma'am. Like I said, I'm a friend."

"Why are you worried about her?"

He dropped his gaze to the porch, left it there a moment before he looked back up. Going for embarrassed and nervous. "I'm in love with your daughter. I must've scared her off when I asked her..." He shrugged. "I know she wanted to reconcile with you guys. I thought maybe..." He swallowed, added another shrug for good measure. "I guess if you've never heard of me, then she must not be here. I'd like to think she'd have mentioned me. So I guess I'll just..." He turned away.

"Wait!"

He forced the triumphant smile into hiding and turned back.

"Please, come in." She stepped aside, and he entered the two-story foyer, let his gaze wander up the curving staircase in front of him. "We can talk in the kitchen."

He followed her down a tiled hallway and into the great room. She indicated a stool at the long bar that separated the kitchen from the family room, and he slid onto it.

"Can I get you something? Coffee, tea?"

"Did Harper learn to make her sweet tea from you?"

The woman's eyes filled, and she blinked the emotion away. "She likes it sweeter than I do."

"I've gotten used to it." Derrick let his polite smile fade as the woman watched. "I'm worried something's happened to her."

"Oh, no." Mrs. Cloud's tears dripped down her cheeks. "If only she'd come home."

Crap. Obviously, the woman was telling the truth. This trip

had been a waste of time and money, unless Mrs. Cloud could give him a hint as to where Harper might've gone.

"I'm sorry." She wiped her tears, filled two glasses with ice, added some tea, and slid one across to him. "I just miss her. I wish she'd come home."

He sipped it, said, "Thanks," and set it on the granite countertop.

"We haven't heard from Harper since...in a while." Her voice faded.

"Since she was incarcerated?"

"You know about that." The woman's tense shoulders relaxed just a bit. "When she called and told us what happened, my husband answered the phone. He was so angry with her that he refused to help her. He told her..." She swallowed, shook her head. "He told her never to call here again. Of course, he's regretted that ever since. I finally convinced him we should go see her. We drove to Nevada, went to the prison."

They'd gone to see her? Harper hadn't said that.

"We should have gone sooner. Right away, but my husband... Anyway, she'd been released before we got there. Paroled." The woman's voice caught. "She didn't even call. We had no idea how to find her. All she had to do was come home. That's all we wanted."

"She thinks you hate her," Derrick said.

"How could I hate my own child?" With tears streaming down her face, she looked both older and more vulnerable than she had just moments before. "Where was she...? I mean, are you from Nevada, or—"

"She and I met in Vegas, and we fell in love. She moved with me to Baltimore last spring."

The woman swallowed, whispered, "Maryland." She pulled a paper towel from a rack near the stovetop and wiped her eyes. "I'm sorry."

"Don't apologize. I miss her too. I'm worried about her. I asked her to marry me, and she just... She didn't say no, but she didn't say yes, either. Just said she needed time. That was a week ago, and I haven't heard from her since. I thought she'd come here, figured she wanted to reconcile with you guys and tell you the good news. Can you think of anyplace else she might have gone?"

Mrs. Cloud shook her head. "I'm sorry. I have no idea. She hasn't lived at home since she was eighteen. I'm sure there are a lot of things in her past we don't know anything about. She lived in LA for a while, and you know about Vegas."

"Maybe other family members?"

"If she'd gone to any of their houses, they'd have told us. Everyone in the family knows how desperate we are to see her again."

A dead end. Derrick let his head loll forward before he looked up again. "I'm sorry I bothered you. I didn't mean to dredge up bad memories."

The woman sniffed. "Not at all. You seem like... I mean, we know her last boyfriend wasn't exactly..." Her words trailed off again.

Derrick ducked his head, smiled slightly. "I hope I'm a better choice. I think that's what scared her away. She's afraid to trust me."

"She's not a great judge of character, especially of men."

"I understand the kind of guys she's been with before. But I'm... Not that I'm a catch or anything. But I have a good job. I don't break the law. I was hoping she and I could buy a house and..." He pursed his lips. "I can't think about that, not until I find her."

"What can I do to help?" Mrs. Cloud asked. "We could hire a PI or something. We've talked about it before, but my husband thought, if she wanted to come home, she'd contact us. But if you think she might be in danger—"

"I don't know that we should assume that yet." Derrick thought about the words Mrs. Cloud hadn't said, the words she'd implied. *We have money.* That might come in handy. First, he had to win their trust, and he figured Harper's dad wouldn't be nearly as easy to win over as her mom had been. "I think she must've just gone somewhere to think things through. Maybe an old vacation spot or something?"

The woman looked toward the ceiling before she met his eyes again. "We used to vacation in Eureka Springs. She loved it there."

Derrick pulled out his cell phone and tapped on an app to take notes. "Where is that?"

"Arkansas. We always rented a cabin on Beaver Lake."

"Do you remember the name of the resort?"

Her slight laugh died fast. "More of a campground than resort. I can't remember the name off the top of my head, but my husband will know."

They exchanged cell phone numbers, and Mrs. Cloud promised to call him with the name of the campground after she'd spoken to her husband.

"And you promise to call us when you find her?" she said.

"Yes, ma'am. As soon as I know she's safe."

"Promise me you'll tell her..." The woman's eyes filled with tears, but she didn't bother to swipe them away. "Tell her how much we miss her. How badly we want her back."

"I promise."

Derrick left the house with the woman's image in his mind. He would find Harper, and he might even tell her what her mother had said. But only after Harper helped him get the money. Otherwise, the woman would have to visit her daughter in the cemetery.

CHAPTER TWENTY-FOUR

Jack transferred the steaks to a platter and covered them with foil.

"Something sure smells good," Red said.

Jack turned as the man shuffled in from the living room and sat at the table. "Steak *au poivre.*"

Red's eyes narrowed. "Sounds froufrou."

"Doesn't smell froufrou, though," Jack said.

"Smells like heaven in a frying pan."

Jack had to agree as he added cream and pepper to the skillet and stirred. While that simmered, he checked the potatoes and vegetables in the oven. It was fun to have someone to cook for. Someone to appreciate him. He'd been cooking for one for too long.

Not that Red was the dinner companion of his dreams. He'd had a few girlfriends in college, but nothing serious. When he'd moved to Nutfield, he'd figured he'd eventually meet the right woman. Until then, he'd focus on saving his pennies and building his real estate business.

Now, it looked like he was well on his way with the business. What about the woman?

He imagined Harper, those beautiful eyes, the way she smiled when she let her guard down. He'd love nothing more than to see that smile every single day of his life.

It was too soon to start thinking of her like that. Way too soon.

Ten minutes later, he prepared two plates and carried them to the table.

Red leaned over his, pulled in a long breath, and said, "I'll give you ten thousand dollars to teach Harper to cook."

Jack laughed as he sat beside him. "You're a tough negotiator, old man."

After they said grace, Jack watched Red cut a small bite, dredge it in the creamy gravy, and pop it in his mouth. His eyes closed as he savored the meat. When they opened again, he said, "Okay, twenty thousand, but that's my final offer."

Twenty thousand dollars to spend time with the woman he was falling for?

His amusement faded as the truth of it settled in his belly with the steak. Yes, he was falling for Harper Cloud. Falling hard. And he couldn't seem to keep his heart in line no matter how many times he told himself he was crazy to even consider getting involved with her.

And it was crazy. The woman had kept as much from him as she'd told him, and he didn't know how much of what she'd told him was the truth. She seemed shrouded in mystery, and not the good kind. The trouble kind.

He knew women like that. Had a sister like that. A sister who couldn't seem to pick the right guys or the right friends or the right jobs. Angel had been arrested so many times, Jack had lost count. A couple of times for drug possession, but she wasn't an addict. Just an idiot. Most of her arrests were for shoplifting. The latest one had been thanks to a check-cashing scheme, and that stunt had landed her in prison. He thought she was still there, but his parents had quit updating him on Angel's latest dramas. He didn't want to hear about it. He prayed for her every day, but that was as much as he intended to be involved in her life. It was sad, and it was wrong, but Jack had very little hope that his baby sister would ever get her life together.

Jack had told himself he'd never become involved with a woman like that.

Did Harper love the rush of life on the edge? Did she thrive on drama like Angel did? She must to some degree. Moving to LA, dancing in Vegas. How else would she have ended up as an entertainer at a strip club? She'd told him the story, and it made sense. But a rational person didn't end up like that.

Rational people grew up and got jobs and reconciled with their families. Or skipped the falling-outs all together.

Which meant there was something off about Harper. And if that were the case, what was he doing letting her into his life?

Was Harper like Angel, though? She seemed down to earth, devoted to her grandfather. She worked hard. She was reliable. Jack couldn't say any of those things about Angel, who'd only ever been devoted to herself and hadn't held down a real job more than a few months at a time.

Maybe Harper wanted normalcy. Maybe, despite the lies and half-truths, she was trying to get her life together. Jack could feel differently about a woman who'd learned from her mistakes, couldn't he?

After the meal, Jack cleaned the kitchen, left a plate of dinner in the fridge for Harper, and joined Red in the living room. He opened a paper bag he'd carried in earlier and pulled out a DVD player.

"What are we gonna do with that?"

"Watch movies," Jack said.

"Don't have any movies."

Jack reached into the bag and grabbed the two DVDs he'd ordered online, which he handed to the old man.

His face broke into a wrinkly smile. "Marilyn Monroe."

"Those are the ones you and Steve were talking about the other day, right?"

"*Gentlemen Prefer Blondes* is my favorite."

"Then we'll watch that first." Jack hunkered down behind the TV with cords.

"Bebe loved Marilyn."

Jack connected the HDMI cord. "Bebe was your wife?"

"Yeah." Red's voice softened. "Lost her eight years ago. Cancer."

"I'm sorry." Jack peeked out from behind the TV. "Must have been rough."

"The worst. At the end, I just wanted to crawl into that hospital bed and go with her."

Jack plugged in the DVD player, scooted out from behind the TV, and sat back on his heels. Seemed Red was in the mood to talk. "I can't imagine."

"I'd thought burying our only child was the worst pain a man could live through. And it had been." Red's eyes filled, but he hardly seemed to notice.

Jack couldn't imagine what had brought on the maudlin mood, but now wasn't the time for a comedy film.

Something didn't make sense though. Their only child? But Harper's father...

"It was a car accident," Red said. "Took him and his wife. Left Derrick." Red's lips pinched closed. Based on the look on the old man's face, Derrick must have been the "idiot grandkid" Red had referenced the day before.

"How old was he when his parents died?" Jack asked.

"College student. Dumb kid had everything he needed, but he took after his dad."

Apparently, that wasn't good.

"Don't get me wrong," Red added. "George was a great guy, a hard worker, decent husband and father. But he had a weakness for the tables."

"Gambling?"

"Died in debt up to his eyeballs. I paid it all off, paid for the rest of Derrick's college, tried to give the kid everything he needed."

Jack had a feeling Derrick hadn't made his grandfather proud.

"He's just like his father," Red said. "Great job, makes all the money he should ever need, and loses it as fast as he can make it." He shook his head. "I thought he'd changed. Thought Harper was having a good influence on him. When I hired her to be my nurse, he started coming around more."

Whoa. Red had *hired* her? Red continued before Jack could fully form the questions materializing in his mind.

"I thought he moved her in to take care of me because he cared about me." He shook his head sadly. "I'm just a stupid old man. I believed him. I wanted to believe him. He's my grandson, you know? I love the kid. And then, he tried to con me out of money. 'To invest,' he told me. Right. I'd raised George, knew all the tricks. I can smell a liar a mile away. Especially when there's money involved. At least George was smart enough to keep all his loans on the up-and-up. Mortgaged to the hilt, but banks don't break your kneecaps."

Jack rubbed his knee. "Surely it wasn't that bad."

Red shrugged. "Harper doesn't know this, but I called him once this summer after I'd refused to give him the money, just to find out the truth. He admitted he was in debt and desperate. Tried to convince me that if he didn't come up with the money, they'd kill him." He harrumphed like only an old man could. "I'm not stupid. If they killed him, they'd get nothing. I told Derrick a broken knee would serve him right."

"Tough love."

"Love. Not sure you could call it that. Fact is, I worked hard for my money. It's not like I can go make more. He's gonna get most of it when I die anyway. He'll probably gamble it away in a year."

"Maybe he'll surprise you."

Red continued as if Jack hadn't spoken. "That's why I wrote Harper into the will. She won't fritter it away. She'll be able to finish college or do whatever she wants with it."

Jack was reeling from all the information. But one thing seemed abundantly clear. "She's not your granddaughter."

Red blinked twice. Narrowed his eyes. Then he smiled for the first time since dinner. "Don't tell anybody. We're supposed to keep that quiet."

"Why?"

"She figured it'd be easier for her to take care of me if people thought we were related. If I need medical attention or something, she can make decisions for me."

"Right," Jack said. But his steak turned over in his stomach. He shifted to a more comfortable position on the floor, took a deep breath, and threw out the next question. Maybe the old man would give him an honest answer. "Why are you two here? Why did you leave Baltimore?"

Red's mouth flattened. "Don't think I'm supposed to say."

"You've told me everything else."

"You got a trustworthy face."

Jack forced a smile. "Gee, thanks."

"You won't hold it against her?"

His stomach tightened even more. Maybe he didn't want to know. But the words "I promise" popped out before he could think it through.

"I don't remember everything that happened, but..." His voice faded, and his eyes narrowed. A moment later, he shook his head. "Anyway, something happened. There's someone from her past she's scared of. I figure it's an old boyfriend. You know about her past. Lotsa checkered fellows back there."

Jack didn't let on how little he knew.

"She told me she had to leave and begged me to go with her."

"Why didn't she just hire you a different nurse?"

"It would have been easier on me. But I couldn't stand the idea of her taking off all by herself. Nobody to look after her. Harper might not be family, but she's the closest thing I got, considering Derrick hasn't come around in months. I was worried about her. I saw some bruises."

Those bruises... An old boyfriend had done that to her? What horrors had Harper suffered at the hands of men? It was no wonder she was suspicious, no wonder she fought to protect herself.

Despite all Jack had learned tonight, a wave of affection rose. An irrational, ridiculous urge to show Harper that not all men were like the ones she'd known before. That a man could love her the way God intended. If only he could help her learn to trust, to be loved...

Whoa. What was he thinking? She'd done nothing but lie to him.

Red stared at the black TV screen a moment. "Someone hurt her. And something happened..."

Red's words faded away, and he stared beyond Jack. The color in his cheeks paled. He swallowed, rubbed his eyes.

Jack stood. "You okay?"

"Something just... I feel like something else happened, something... but I can't remember." He shook his head and focused on Jack. "My brain..." He tapped the side of his head three times. "I used to be able to rely on it. It's turning against me. Now, I never know if I can trust what I remember. All I know is, I don't remember enough." He took a deep breath. "But I trust Harper. She said she had to go, so here we are."

Jack tried to process all Red had told him, tried to reconcile the information with the stories Harper had told him. Who was after her? The ex who'd gone to prison? The big-shot dance club owner who'd had her fired? Or was this problem related to the *this and that* she'd neglected to tell him about? "So you guys just took off? What did your grandson think about that?"

Red's scoff told Jack as much as his words. "All he cares about is my money." Red sighed and sat back in his recliner. "Seems unbelievable, I know, but I miss that idiot grandson of mine."

"He's your only connection to your son. He's your family."

"That's right." Red nodded a few times. His eyes filled again. "Haven't talked to him in weeks. Harper keeps saying we'll call him, but he never answers his phone." Red nodded to the TV. "We gonna watch that movie or what?"

Jack finished connecting the DVD player while he mulled over all he'd learned. One thing still didn't make sense.

He kept his focus on the TV. "You have money, right? You didn't give it to Derrick."

"Of course I didn't. I just told you that." He huffed a long breath. "And they say I have memory issues."

Jack slid in the DVD, waited for it to load.

"I started forgetting stuff," Red said. "Least that's what Harper told me. So I turned over power of attorney to my lawyer, an old friend of mine. That way Derrick couldn't swindle it out of me."

Jack had witnessed the dementia, so he knew that part of the story was real. He turned on the TV, pressed the button to bring up the video, and tried to sound casual. "So how come Harper has to work so hard to pay the bills?"

When Red didn't answer, Jack turned to face him. The man's eyes were scrunched up like he was thinking. "You know what, son? I don't rightly know."

CHAPTER TWENTY-FIVE

It was after ten when Harper got home. She pushed open the door to find Jack seated on the sofa, staring at the TV. Gramps's chair was empty.

"How was your night?" she asked.

He didn't return her smile. "Interesting."

What did that mean? She closed the door behind her and crossed to the kitchen. "Was Gramps okay?"

"He's tucked in bed."

"Sorry I'm late."

Jack clicked off the TV and joined her. "You're right on time." Still no smile. Maybe he got grouchy when he was sleepy.

"Thanks for staying with him." She opened the refrigerator, saw a plate covered with plastic wrap. Was that...? "You made steak?"

"Yup." He leaned against the door jamb and crossed his arms.

She pulled out the plate, took the plastic wrap off, and inhaled the scent. "That smells divine. You mind if I eat in front of you?"

"I ate."

She paused halfway to the microwave and turned. "What's wrong?"

"Red and I had a long chat tonight."

Uh-oh. She set the plate on the table, her appetite quickly fading. "About what?"

"This and that. Like how you're not really his granddaughter."

She lowered herself into a chair.

Jack didn't move.

"I just…" She forced herself to make eye contact, but it wasn't easy the way Jack was glowering at her. "I'm his nurse, and he's given me… I can get out the paper that gives me the right to make medical decisions for him. But it's easier—"

"Why are you here?"

Her empty stomach filled with acid. Could she trust Jack with this? Would he believe her?

She nodded to the chair beside her. "Can you sit down please?"

He eyed the chair.

She pushed away the cold plate, clasped her shaking hands together in her lap.

"Derrick—"

"Your boyfriend."

"Ex." She said it too fast, as if it mattered. As if Jack would care, which, after this, he obviously wouldn't. Not about her, not that way. "He's been my ex for a while. He has a problem."

"Gambling."

What *hadn't* Gramps told him? "He owes a lot of money."

"To loan sharks," Jack said. "They want their money, and Red wouldn't bail Derrick out."

She nodded, prayed for wisdom. Would he believe her, or would he turn her in?

She met his eyes, saw the determination there. And the anger. "Gramps doesn't know everything," she said.

His eyebrows lifted. "He thinks he does."

"I didn't tell him the truth."

Jack crossed his arms. "At least I'm not the only one. You've lied to me about everything. You lied to 'Gramps'"—his air quotes told her what he thought about that—"so why should I believe you now?"

A wave of irritation—or was it fear?—had her pushing back in her chair. "What makes you think you deserve the truth from me? You're my landlord. I don't have to tell you anything."

He blinked. "I've done nothing but—"

"Yeah, I know. You've helped and helped." Here it came, what she'd been waiting for. His demands for repayment. Tell him everything, and then he'd have even more of a hold over her. Then he'd be able to use it all against her. She stood, backed away until she bumped into the countertop. "And now it's time to pay up? Because that's what every other man I've ever known has told me. How much I owe them for their kindness." Her voice cracked. *Stupid, stupid Harper.* She'd known this would happen.

She'd thought Jack was different.

"Harper, I would never—"

"Kindness is never free. Never."

His hands lifted, palms out. "I didn't—"

"I'll come up with the money to pay you back for...for whatever you think I owe you. Your time, your energy, that ramp outside. Whatever. But I won't... I can't..." She waved at the air, at the expectations she knew he had.

"What do you think I'm asking for?"

"More than I can give."

"Just the truth."

"And then you'll know everything. And then what will you want? What will you demand?"

"Nothing."

Right. Like she could believe that. "We'll be gone in the morning."

"What?" He stepped back, hands still lifted. "No. Wait. You don't have to—"

"We're paid through the end of the month. You can take what I owe you out of that. If you think there's more—"

"You don't owe me money. You don't owe me anything."

Tears burned her eyes, and she looked away. She couldn't tell him the truth. She couldn't trust him. She couldn't trust anybody. "Just go."

"Harper, I'm not trying—"

"What's going on here?" Red's shout had them both turning.

The old man stood in the doorway. His pajamas were wrinkled, his eyes bloodshot and rimmed in dark circles. He leaned heavily on his walker with one hand and pointed a gnarly finger at Jack with the other. "What did you do?"

Jack's hands were still up. "I was just asking her—"

"You hurt that girl"—Red shook his finger—"I'll take you out."

"I would never..." Jack's eyes were wide, his mouth open.

Harper looked back at Gramps. The color had drained from his face, making his red eyes look even worse. "We're okay," she said. "Everything's fine. We were just talking."

"Talking loud enough to wake the dead." He glared at Jack.

"We're okay." She crossed toward the old man. Jack had to step out of the way so she could pass. She was careful to leave plenty of space between them. "I'm sorry we woke you."

Another moment passed before he jerked his walker back toward the hallway. "Had to use the bathroom anyway."

She followed him into the hall and waited outside the bathroom door, then escorted him back to his bedroom and got him settled. He seemed hardly awake as he rested his head on his pillow.

"Are you all right?" she asked.

"I heard yelling. I thought... I thought..."

"You thought I was in trouble. I understand. You were protecting me." She patted his shoulder. "And I love you for it." She reached for the lamp, but he stopped her with a hand on her arm.

"Did he hurt you?"

She shook her head. Of course Jack was frustrated with her. She'd lied to him. A lot. And now she'd overreacted. Accused him of... Shame burned her cheeks. What was wrong with her?

"I told Jack stuff tonight," Gramps said.

"I figured that out."

"I didn't mean to make trouble for you. But I think we should trust him." His lids drifted shut. When he said nothing else, she switched the light off and left him to sleep.

She found Jack pulling a plate from the microwave. The room was filled with the scent of meat and pepper and roasted vegetables. He set the plate on the table. "I think you need to eat."

She tried to come up with a witty response, but her stomach spoke for her with a growl.

Jack's lips twitched. "*Hangry* much?"

She snatched a fork and knife from the drawer and sat. The first bite of steak melted in her mouth. She couldn't help the "Mmm" as she cut the second.

Jack slid a glass of water onto the table, then stood behind his chair and curled his hands over the top.

She swallowed her third bite while she tried to figure out what to say. What to do.

She couldn't trust this man.

She couldn't *not* trust him, either. Because despite her big pronouncement earlier, they had nowhere to go and no money to get there.

"You might as well sit," she said.

"Your... Red... is pretty angry with me. Maybe I should go."

"He won't remember any of this tomorrow."

Jack blew out a long breath. "You don't owe me anything. My kindness doesn't come with a price tag."

"Gramps..." She took a deep breath, started again. "Red doesn't believe in debt. Did he tell you that?"

Jack didn't respond. Didn't sit. Just studied her as if he were trying to solve a puzzle. Eyes hooded, mouth closed, fists clenched over the chair.

"He doesn't believe in consumer debt, anyway," she said. "He'll take out a loan to buy a property but nothing else."

She met his gaze, waited for a response. Finally, he said, "Okay."

"He does believe there's something we should all owe."

"Which is?" Jack asked.

She nodded to the chair again. "Sit down, and I'll tell you."

He sat, back straight, hands clasped together on the table.

"He says, 'The only thing you should ever owe is love.'"

Jack blinked, tilted his head to the side.

She shrugged, ate another bite of her dinner, sipped her water. "I guess it's from the Bible."

"'Owe no man anything, but to love one another,'" Jack said. "It's in Romans."

Jack knew the reference? If that wasn't confirmation that she should trust him, she didn't know what was. "So I do owe you something, don't I?"

"You really—"

"I don't think it's possible to..." She faltered, looked away. "It's impossible to love your neighbor..." There, that sounded non-romantic, right? She met his eyes again. "When you're telling so many lies."

He nearly smiled. "Good point."

"I'm not good at trusting people."

"Not even Red, apparently."

"What? No. I trust him completely."

"You just said he doesn't know the whole story. So you must not."

"Oh. That." She took a deep breath, speared a bite of potato. It was delicious, but she'd already eaten more than she should this late at night. She pushed the plate to the center of the table and sipped from the water Jack had given her.

He glanced at the plate. "You're not done already, are you?"

"It's a lot."

He eyed the steak, and she couldn't help but chuckle. "Go on. You know you want to."

"I'm not proud." He pulled it toward him and cut a piece for himself.

"Typical man."

His amusement faded. "I hope what you think is 'typical' for a man isn't true of me."

She felt her cheeks burn. The last thing she wanted was to return to this conversation. "I just meant..."

When she didn't finish, he said, "Yeah, I know."

He finished off her dinner in about five minutes, then pushed back in his chair.

She stood before he could, grabbed the dirty dish, and set it in the sink.

"You don't have to tell me anything," he said. "You're right. It's none of my business, and you don't owe me anything."

She wanted to tell him. But what if he didn't believe her? There was too much to lose. Not just the tenuous life they'd made here in Nutfield, but the connection she and Jack had forged. She didn't want to lose that. She didn't want to lose Jack.

He stood, pushed in his chair. He glanced at the doorway, then focused on her again.

Their gazes met, though neither spoke.

The air between them pulsed.

Neither moved. She knew she should look away, but she couldn't seem to force herself to. Here was a man who'd done nothing but help her. Who'd been kind to her and Gramps. Here was a man who cooked for her and served her. How could she not want to be with a man like him?

He crossed the room toward her. She should step back, out of his reach, but her feet weren't cooperating. Or maybe they were listening to her heart, not her head, because there was something reassuring in his movements.

He took her hands in his. When he met her eyes, he was so close, she could feel his breath in her hair.

She had to stop this, now. Before it went too far. But she didn't have the strength.

She'd never had the strength.

He bent his head, his gaze flitting from her eyes to her lips. He was going to kiss her. A kiss was supposed to mark the beginning of something good.

But for her, every kiss had been the beginning of a downward spiral that led to her destruction.

A descent into drugs.

A prison sentence.

A horrifying assault in a parking lot.

And now, this.

But Jack didn't know any of that. His lips brushed hers.

She told herself not to, but as always, her body refused to obey. She kissed him back, feeling his hunger, his need. Every cell in her body responded to that need.

Her arms slid around his neck, her mouth opened, and her self-control disappeared.

This kiss was more powerful than any she'd experienced before. Which meant the fallout would be devastating.

She pushed him away.

He stepped back, eyes wide. "I shouldn't have—"

"You need to go."

He blinked, and his gaze filled with sadness, worry, regret.

She understood that last one. She'd live to regret that kiss. This time, she might never recover.

"I'm sorry," he said. "You don't owe me anything."

Her laugh was short and joyless. "Right."

"I promise. I'm not—"

"Go. Now."

He watched her, his eyes pleading, begging. For what, she wished she didn't know. But she did know what he wanted, and she knew exactly what it would cost to give it to him.

"I'm sorry." He turned, walked toward the front door. She didn't move, couldn't bring herself to watch him leave.

The door opened, then closed with a soft click.

CHAPTER TWENTY-SIX

Jack set his egg-and-sausage burrito on the kitchen table beside his coffee and opened his laptop.

He'd run a credit check on Harper before he'd rented her the house, and he'd found nothing that bothered him. He'd called her previous landlord in Las Vegas, who'd confirmed that she'd always paid her rent on time and never caused any trouble. What else had he needed to know?

Nothing then. And nothing now.

Because her life was none of his business. She'd made that very clear the night before when she'd ordered him out of the house.

He swallowed a sip of coffee and tried not to think about that kiss.

It was just a kiss. And he shouldn't have done it. He'd known it was a mistake even as he'd crossed the room.

What an idiot. Red and Harper meant so much to him, but when he stripped away his emotions and looked at the core of the situation, he remembered that they were renters. His first renters, and he'd totally blown it. What if Harper reported him for sexual harassment or something?

The thought didn't take root. Even after everything, he didn't think she was the type. Not vindictive. Not vengeful.

Just suspicious.

And people who were suspicious of others were often the ones others needed to be suspicious of.

If that even made sense.

He opened a browser window, clicked in the search bar.

Hesitated.

Bit into the burrito. The spicy pork sausage and salty cheddar cheese were the perfect accompaniment to the eggs. He had another bite.

Finished the whole thing.

Sipped his coffee while he glanced at the news on his homepage. Typical political junk. Why couldn't people just get along? Be nice, for crying out loud? Be honest?

Harper had been anything but honest.

She was absolutely not the type of woman he should fall for.

Should have fallen for, he amended, because he was already careening toward a crash landing. And there wasn't a thing he could do about it.

All the lies, all the deception, all the suspicion didn't change who she was beneath that hard shell.

He'd felt the truth in her kiss. In the way her arms had slid around his neck. The way her lips had parted, soft and eager and—

Not going there.

Right.

This was ridiculous.

He found a website that would do a national background check for thirty bucks. Paid the money and typed her name.

He hit enter before he could talk himself out of it.

He watched the progress bar inch to the right, his slow internet practically huffing with the effort. Only a handful of results were returned. It just took a second to find the listing for his Harper.

His Harper. Like that was ever going to happen.

He clicked, watched the progress bar again. Sipped his coffee. Hated himself.

What kind of man did a background check on the woman he...

Nope. He had to shut his stupid brain up.

And then, results.

He set down the coffee and stared at the screen.

His hands trembled. It couldn't be.

More clicks, more searches. He read the stories. A man had been killed in a liquor store robbery.

Three people had gone to prison for the murder.

Harper Cloud was a convicted felon.

THIS AND THAT.

The words kept running through Jack's mind as he showered and prepared for his day. The words Harper had used to describe the time between when her boyfriend had been sent to prison and the time she'd moved to Maryland.

This and that.

Jack couldn't get the situation, or the woman, out of his mind.

Because *this and that* referred to prison.

She'd been in prison.

That sweet, beautiful woman had been an accessory to murder?

It couldn't be. Surely she'd been wrongfully convicted.

He couldn't wrap his mind around it. So he focused on something else.

After some back-and-forth negotiating the day before, the sellers had accepted his offer on the twenty-four-unit complex, and he needed to sign the paperwork. He and Ginny had planned to meet at McNeal's—his idea. A very bad one, in retrospect.

He called Ginny and asked if they could meet at her office instead. Because Harper would be at McNeal's, and he couldn't see her right now.

He didn't want to.

Or at least, he didn't want to want to. Which wasn't exactly the same thing, but nobody was splitting hairs.

He arrived at the Realtor's office and was ushered to a large conference room, where he took a seat on the far side of the long table.

Ginny came in a moment later carrying a thin file. "Congratulations!" She held out her hand, and he shook it.

"Thanks."

By the look on her face, he hadn't exhibited the enthusiasm she'd anticipated. He tried to muster it up. "I'm looking forward to making it mine."

She sat beside him, opened the file, and slid the contract around for him to see. "Trouble in paradise?"

He looked up. "I'm sorry?"

She looked at him with raised eyebrows. "You and your whaler girlfriend." She grinned. "You know. Harpoon. Harper..." She watched his face, and the grin faded. "Sorry. Just kidding."

"She's not my girlfriend."

Ginny put back on her professional face. "Right. If you'll just sign here"—she pointed to a line—"and here."

He signed those two and the other places she indicated, then set the pen down. "I really appreciate—"

"Look, I'm—"

They'd spoken at the same time, then stopped. He nodded to her.

She swallowed, took a deep breath. "Your love life is none of my business. I'm trying..." Her voice faded, and then she forced the corners of her mouth up, though nobody would call it a smile. "I haven't lived in Nutfield very long, and I don't know very many people."

When she trailed off, he said, "I'm sorry. That must be hard."

"I moved to Nutfield because my sister lives here. She's married, has kids. My dad died, and Mom's not exactly... Well, my sister's the only family I've got. But they're busy. And I'm just..." She dropped her head into her hands and sighed. Then she looked back up with a plastic smile. "I'm trying to make this work. I'm trying to make friends. That's all that was—me trying to be friendly. But what I said was inappropriate."

Jack was so shocked by Ginny's gush of honesty that he couldn't think of a word to say. He considered taking her hand, because he understood loneliness. He understood that deep, aching need to be seen, to be touched. To have contact with another human being, one who cared. He'd lived it. Was living it. The couple of weeks he'd spent with Red and Harper were an aberration in his otherwise solitary life.

He didn't take her hand, though. Instead, he patted it, then sat back. Safe, friendly. Nothing else. "You aren't wrong about Harper and me. At least, I wouldn't have thought you were wrong yesterday."

Her eyes narrowed the tiniest bit as she studied him. "You care for her."

"I do. If nothing else, she's a friend."

A look passed over her face, and he realized what he'd said. "You're a friend, too, Ginny. I'm just a guy, so I don't talk about my feelings and stuff." He smiled, shrugged. "But I'd like to think we're friends."

Her face brightened, and if he wasn't mistaken, he thought he saw tears fill her eyes.

Sheesh, he had to get out of there.

Because as pretty as Ginny was—and she was quite attractive— she held nothing on the damaged, lonely, frightened woman who'd stolen his heart.

And been involved in a man's murder.

Ginny composed herself, gathered the papers. "Well. Okay, then." She stood and held the papers against her chest like a shield. "So, you'll let me know when you get the inspection scheduled? I'd like to be there."

He pushed back his chair and stood as well. "Definitely. And about the other thing—"

"It's fine," she said. "I'll make friends. These things take time."

He left her office with his copies of the contract and considered the odd conversation he'd just had. Ginny was a woman with a college degree and a real estate license. She had coworkers and clients and family. And yet, she was struggling to make her way in a new town.

How could somebody like Harper, somebody with no degree, little work experience, and a felony on her record, ever make it?

Why was she here?

That was the question that plagued him. Why would she bring Red, not even a relative, and leave the comfort and familiarity of his Maryland home to barely scrape by living in a shack in New Hampshire?

It made no sense.

And when he added the felony conviction to the list of things he knew about her, suddenly her being in New Hampshire felt sinister.

What was Harper Cloud doing?

Why was she hiding?

Who was she hiding from?

———————

CHAPTER TWENTY-SEVEN

Derrick paced at his gate at the Charlotte, NC, airport. He'd arrived in Eureka Springs the day before, trolled the campground Harper's family had visited as a child.

No sign of her. Not at the campground, not at the nearest grocery store, not anywhere.

People didn't forget a face like Harper's. A beautiful woman with an old man? If she'd been there, surely someone would have remembered her. Unless she'd rented a house from a private owner.

She could be less than a mile away or anywhere in the US.

Derrick didn't think she was in Arkansas. Even if she were, he'd never be able to find her on his own. So he was on his way back to Baltimore. His best chance was to go back to Tank and hire him to track her down. And then hope Tank cooperated when he found her. Derrick couldn't have Gramps's attorney—or the cops— knowing Derrick had located the two of them.

Over the loudspeaker, the gate agent began pre-boarding his flight. He was itching to get on the plane. This entire trip had been a waste of time, time Harper'd undoubtedly been using to make herself invisible.

His cell rang, and he glanced at the screen. He didn't recognize the number or the area code. "Derrick Burns."

"Son? Is that you?"

He gripped the phone as if it might escape. "Gramps?"

"Aha! I knew Harper was dialing the wrong number. How are you, son?"

Derrick took a deep breath. He had to tread very carefully here. "I'm doing well. Missing you guys, though. When do you think you'll be home?"

"Not anytime soon, I'm sorry to say. Not that I don't like it here."

"Sure. Of course." *Think, Derrick.* What would she have told him? Surely Gramps didn't know he wasn't supposed to call. "What's the name of the town again?"

"Uh... I don't remember. Something funny."

"Oh. Which state are you in?"

"We're up north."

That didn't exactly narrow it down. The gate agent made another announcement, and Derrick paced toward a quieter space on the far side of the corridor.

"It's cold here," Gramps continued. "We went to the coast the other day. Friend of ours drove us. Pretty coastline. Real rugged. Your grandmother would've loved it."

"A friend? Does Harper know people there?"

"Don't think she did 'til we got here."

So she'd just chosen some random spot? He doubted that. "Must be hard being all alone. I wish you two would come home. What made you decide to leave?"

"I thought she told you all this."

"She wasn't really speaking to me."

There was a long pause, then, "Hold on a sec. Lemme get somewhere private."

Derrick heard the man's heavy breathing, the rattle of the walker, the slam of a door.

"Where are you, Gramps?"

"The rec center. I was playing cards with Steve, and he got a call on his cell, and I thought, I'm gonna borrow his phone and try calling Derrick myself. I remembered a long time ago you gave me one of your business cards, and I put it in my wallet. I looked, and there it was."

Steve. A rec center. A little house somewhere up north in a town with a funny name. "I'm glad you found it. I've been worried about you two. I've tried to call, but Harper's phone always goes to voice mail."

"That so? She's always got it on her. But it doesn't work real well."

"Any chance you know her phone number?"

"Someone here probably has it. Want me to ask?"

That didn't seem like a good idea. Somebody could tip her off. And then she'd run again, taking his grandfather with her. Rage rolled over him like a Las Vegas wind.

"Anyway." Gramps lowered his voice. "Some guy roughed her up pretty bad."

Not as badly as Derrick would once he got ahold of her. His ribs still throbbed after his meeting with Quentin. Her fault. All her fault. "I knew about the bruises. But why did that make her want to leave?"

"She was afraid whoever did it would come back, finish her off. And I didn't want her to be all alone."

He'd never known Harper to be a liar, but she'd worked that one out pretty fast.

"There was something else, too," Gramps said. "Something… But I don't remember exactly. Something bad."

What? When Derrick had left her that night at Gramps's house, he'd had no reason to believe she'd run away. And then, they'd been gone. Why? What had changed?

A memory filtered back. Quentin's remark about the goons who'd beat Harper up going missing. Derrick had suggested that maybe she'd done something to them, but that had only been a defense mechanism. He'd never considered it could have been true. Sweet Harper couldn't hurt anyone. But now... What if she'd killed them?

How could she have? Keith wouldn't have shown his face. Probably neither had the other guy. She wouldn't have known how to find them, even if she did have it in her to kill somebody. Which she didn't, he was sure, despite the felony conviction.

Maybe Keith and the other goon had gone to the house.

When he'd been there Monday, had anything been out of place?

He thought back. He'd been so focused on talking to her, but he hadn't seen anything that raised alarms.

Except... The deadbolt on the back door had been unlocked. Odd, but not too much so. He hadn't worried they'd been kidnapped, not with the cars gone. He'd thought it an oversight.

"You still there, son?" Gramps asked.

"She must have been terrified to take off the way she did."

"She was," Gramps said. "I had to come with her. You understand, right? You don't come around very much, so I figured you wouldn't miss me—"

"I do miss you, though. I miss you a lot."

"That's mighty kind of you to say, son. I miss you, too."

Derrick remembered his plan from earlier that week. Mend fences with Gramps. Get in his good graces again. He forced himself to add, "And I'm sorry about what happened this summer. About the investment and... all that."

After a moment, Gramps said, "I'm proud of you for saying that. And of course I forgive you."

Derrick barely kept himself from scoffing. Forgiveness. If Gramps cared a whit about him, he'd have given him the money, and they wouldn't be in this situation now. "Thank you. That means a lot."

"You get all that mess worked out?" Gramps asked.

Right. Like two hundred grand had just dropped into his lap. "Yeah. Thanks for asking."

"Good. Good to hear it." He didn't sound convinced, but at

least he didn't push it. "And anyway, I don't blame you for not coming around more. You've got a life. Friends and work. Harper... She hasn't got anybody. I didn't want her to be alone. So I offered to come with her until all this stuff was cleared up."

"How's that going?"

Gramps was quiet. Derrick paced to the windows and stared out at the airplanes on the tarmac, forcing himself not to speak. Finally, Gramps huffed out a breath. "She's always on that danged phone looking at websites. But I don't know exactly what she's looking for. Whatever it is, I don't think she's found it."

What could she possibly have been hoping to find? "I miss you guys. I'd like to come see you."

"I'm not giving you any money, son."

"I know." Derrick forced a smile into his voice. "I don't need it. I just want to make sure you two are okay."

"I guess that'd be all right."

"But I need to know where you are exactly, and I don't have Harper's phone number. Do you think you could get your address for me and call me back?"

"Sure. Of course."

But then he'd have to wait, and who knew when—or if—Gramps would call back. And of course he'd tell Harper they'd talked.

"Better yet," he said, "can I ask a favor?"

Another long pause. Derrick interrupted this one with, "I promise, I'm not asking for money."

"What is it then?"

"Are you on an iPhone?"

"How in the blazes should I know?"

Derrick took a deep breath. "Can you put me on speaker? Look at the phone. And press the button that says speaker."

Seconds ticked by while Gramps muttered. A moment later, he said, "Did it."

"Great. Now, I want you to go to the messages app. It looks like a little dialog balloon. You know what I mean? Like in comics?"

"I'm not that old," Gramps said. "Done."

"Start a new text to me." Derrick recited his phone number as he walked the corridor to the bank of screens that displayed departures and arrivals.

"Done," Gramps said.

Derrick led his grandfather through the process of sending his current location. It took forever, lots of starts and stops, but finally, it worked.

Derrick studied the map on the cell phone. They were in Nutfield, New Hampshire.

"Got it." He looked up at the screens with all the flight information. And there it was. A direct flight to Manchester. He could be there in a few hours.

He looked around, spotted an airline service counter, and started in that direction.

Derrick's heart pounded. He had her. Now, he had to make sure she wouldn't get away before he could get there. "One more thing. Please, don't tell Harper we talked. I want to surprise her. And... Well, I think you know this already. I'm in love with her, Gramps, but I blew it."

Gramps harrumphed like only an old man could. "I'm sorry to say, son, but I think you did." He was quiet again. The man was never in a hurry. Must be nice. Derrick made eye contact with the woman behind the counter. She stood waiting for him, so he gestured to his phone, rolled his eyes, and mouthed an apology. Never hurt to be charming.

"I almost lost your grandmother once," Gramps said. "We were dating, and I acted like a jerk. She swore she was finished with me. But I wooed her back. Brought my old guitar and sat outside her folks' house and serenaded her." His laugh was somehow both happy and sad. "Sang *Earth Angel* at her window until she opened it up."

"I didn't know you could sing."

He chuckled. "Can't sing, and I was terrible on that guitar. I always wondered if she just came outside to shut me up before the neighbors started throwing stuff."

Derrick couldn't imagine his grandparents young and in love, though they'd definitely been *old* and in love until Gram died.

"I want to do something like that. I want to surprise her with a big, romantic gesture."

"Then I won't warn her you're coming. But on winning her back...you might have some competition."

Derrick's heart pounded a war beat. "What do you mean?"

"She's got a fellow up here. Not sure they're an item yet, but they seem to like each other."

Derrick swallowed his anger and said, "Uh-oh. What his name?"

"Jack."

Jack. Derrick would remember that. "Well then," he said, "I guess I'd better bring my A-game."

He ended the call, approached the counter, and smiled at the woman behind it. "My grandfather. Never in a hurry."

"I got one just like that," she said. "What can I do for you?"

"I have to change my flight. I was headed to Baltimore, but there's a family emergency, and I need to get to Manchester right away."

She clicked away on her keyboard, looked up, and smiled. "That flight leaves in forty-five minutes, and there are seats available. Seems like it's your lucky day."

CHAPTER TWENTY-EIGHT

Harper hadn't spoken to Jack all day Thursday.

She kept waiting for him to come by, kept thinking she'd run into him at McNeal's, but he'd kept his distance.

What did that mean? Had he lost interest in her? Or was he trying to learn more about her past?

She thought of little else all day Thursday and into Friday. It was nearly noon when Harper saw the two uniformed police officers on the sidewalk outside the window at work. Cops came into McNeal's all the time. She'd gotten used to them. But after Wednesday night, after the conversation with Jack... She was a fool for still being here. Red had told Jack too much. And her behavior could only have fueled his suspicions. Jack would do some research on her, and then he'd know just enough to think she was up to no good.

The police officers came in. One made eye contact with her. She'd never seen this one before. Not a regular. He was here for her. He recognized her. Why else would he be watching her so closely? He smiled, his eyes crinkling at the corners. What did that mean? Happy he'd found her? Big collar for the day?

His smile faded, and his eyes narrowed.

Bonnie walked past her, brushing her shoulder and whispering a vehement, "Get to work." Then, she focused on the men at the door. "Sit anywhere, guys. The usual?"

The cops chose a table.

Harper spun and headed for the kitchen.

At a table against the far wall, a woman lifted her hand to get Harper's attention. She wanted nothing more than to bolt, but she had to act normally, so she beelined in that direction.

The woman was sitting alone. She had long brown hair and kind eyes. "I'm going to order for myself and my husband. He's running a little late."

Harper took out her order pad. "Okay. What can I get you?"

The woman rattled off the orders. When she was finished, she cocked her head to the side. "You look a little pale today."

Harper had served this woman before many times. She'd always been kind, and she'd never been nosy. Of course today would be the day she'd pry. "I think I've caught a bug or something."

"Oh, dear." The woman smiled. "I'm Samantha, by the way. Most people call me Sam." She held out her hand.

The restaurant door opened. Harper cut her gaze that way. She didn't see a face, just the height of a man who carried himself like a cop. She had to get out of there.

She shook Sam's hand. "Harper Cloud." The tall man approached, and Harper cringed, waited for a hand to clamp down on her shoulder, a set of cuffs to be fastened on her wrists.

Samantha's gaze shifted from friendly to concerned as she glanced from the man to Harper.

Behind her, the man said, "Pardon me."

Harper jumped, stepped out of the way.

"I didn't meant to startle you." The man smiled down at her, then slid into the booth across from Sam.

Right. This was the husband. Another cop. He had to be, the way he carried himself. They were everywhere.

She nodded, spun, and bolted into the kitchen.

She was leaning against the counter, trying to slow her heart rate, when Bonnie walked in. "What is wrong with you today?"

"I just…" She shook her head, tried to think.

"First, the uniforms in the door, then you jump out of your skin at the sight of Garrison, who's in here three, four times a week. What is your problem?"

"Garrison startled me. And the other one, the cop in the doorway, looked familiar. I was trying to place him." Her excuses sounded feeble, and Bonnie was too smart to fall for them. Harper gave the cook the orders she's just gotten from Samantha.

The older woman let out a snort. "You aren't supposed to place 'em. You're supposed to seat 'em and serve 'em. That's your job."

"I know. I'm—"

"You been in another world for two days. I shoulda got someone else for your shift. I think I worked you too hard this week."

"I'm sorry. I'll try harder." The cook slid one plate across the stainless counter. Harper waited for the second in the order while Bonnie watched her through narrowed eyes.

Now Bonnie was suspicious, too. Harper used to think she was a good actor. Apparently not, since everyone could see right through her to the terror she was trying so hard to hide. Suspicion was mounting on all sides. There was no more time to waste. She had to get Red and leave town. Now.

"Actually," Harper said. "I don't feel well. Do you mind if I take off early?"

CHAPTER TWENTY-NINE

Jack had kept his distance from Harper and Red, but his mind was never far from them. He didn't know much, but he did know Harper was in trouble. And as much as he'd tried to help, he'd probably only made everything worse.

The conversation from Wednesday night plagued him as he drove toward the lake. He'd planned to work on one of the rentals today, thinking the manual labor would do him good. He needed to get Harper out of his mind.

He'd kissed her. He shouldn't have done that. But the kiss wasn't what bothered him right now. She'd told him more than she'd planned to, thanks to Red opening up. She'd let her guard down and had been almost honest with him. And then she'd erected those walls again and ordered him out.

Would she suspect he'd dig into her background? If she knew, what would she do?

The answer to that question had him making a quick U-turn and heading toward Nutfield. Because he suddenly had the very strong suspicion he knew exactly what she'd do.

She'd run.

Jack would go straight to the house, except Harper was probably working. He'd check McNeal's first, see if she was there. He had to talk to her, to... he didn't know what. Keep her from leaving, promise to help her with whatever it was she was running from.

How had he gotten himself into this, anyway? Whatever *this* was?

He screeched to a stop outside McNeal's and rushed inside. He scanned the restaurant, saw Bonnie on the far side. The tables were almost all occupied, people eating and drinking and laughing and chatting. Everything seemed normal.

Harper wasn't there.

She could be in the back, though. Maybe.

Bonnie disappeared into the kitchen.

He spotted Samantha Kopp, who waved from a table against the far wall. Sam was one of the property owners he worked for, someone he'd known for years. He walked that direction, noticed her husband Garrison, and gave them both a quick nod.

"Want to join us?" Sam asked.

"No. I'm just..." He glanced toward the kitchen. Where was Harper?

"Too distracted to finish sentences," Garrison suggested.

Jack glanced at the man.

Garrison wore a wry smile. "You're looking for the pretty waitress?"

"Harper," Sam said. "She went in the back a couple of minutes ago." She slid over on the bench seat and patted it. "Join us until she comes back out."

Well, that was a better option than standing there. He slid into the booth.

"What's her story?" Garrison asked. "I've seen her before, and she's always seemed shy, but today she jumped out of her skin when I walked up."

"She said she didn't feel well," Sam said. "She was white as a sheet." She focused on Jack. "Has she been sick?"

Before he could answer, Garrison said, "She didn't seem sick. She seemed scared."

"You think?" Sam tilted her head to the side. "It was right after those two uniformed police officers came in."

Garrison leveled his gaze on Jack's. "What do you know about her?"

"Nothing, really. She's my tenant."

Garrison's eyes narrowed. Jack had always found the man to be kind and funny, but right now, he was every bit his former-FBI self. "You're a terrible liar. How long have you known her?"

"About ten days."

"Has she done something wrong?" Garrison asked.

Jack was afraid to look away and afraid not to. And more than a little irritated that he couldn't answer that question with a definitive *no*.

When Jack didn't answer, Garrison said, "What's her name?"

"Harper," Jack said.

"Last name?"

"I don't—"

"Cloud." Sam said the last name, then shrugged. "She just told me. It's unusual, isn't it? Where's she from?"

Garrison seemed to be waiting for an answer to that question, too. When Jack said nothing, Garrison pulled out his cell phone and typed into it. "I love a unique name. So easy to look up."

"Don't do that," Jack said. "She hasn't done anything wrong."

"Call me eternally curious," Garrison said. "Her actions and your evasiveness suggest something different."

"I'm not being evasive."

"That's what every evasive suspect says."

"I don't know anything." Jack tried to keep his voice level, but worry laced his words.

Garrison said, "They all say that, too."

"She's a tenant." Jack threw that out as nonchalantly as possible. "A pretty one, so yeah, maybe I came here to see her, but nothing else."

Garrison didn't look up from his phone. "I don't even have to see your eyes to know you're lying. Seriously, don't ever try to run a con."

He had no idea how to answer that. How had this conversation gotten out of control so fast? "I think I'm just going to catch up—"

"Hey, Jack." Bonnie approached the table and set plates down in front of Garrison and Sam. The scents of corned beef and french fries filled his nostrils and made his stomach churn. "You here to eat or to stalk my waitress?" She smiled as she said it, but Jack couldn't return the gesture.

Garrison hadn't looked up from his phone at her approach.

Sam was watching her husband with a tilted head and narrowed eyes.

"Is she here?" Jack asked Bonnie.

"Took off a few minutes ago. She said she didn't feel well. There's something off about that girl. She's been distracted for days."

Garrison slid out of the booth, causing Bonnie to sidestep out of his way. He looked down at Jack. All business.

"Don't go anywhere." Garrison marched through the room and out the front door.

Bonnie watched him leave before turning back to them. "The whole town's taking crazy pills today. You need something?"

Jack swallowed rising nausea. Something was really wrong. "No, thanks."

She walked away, shaking her head.

Jack slid out of the booth and stood, but Sam stopped him with a hand on his wrist. "Garrison said not to leave."

"Am I required to do as he says?"

She glanced toward the front door. "He must have a reason."

"I need to go."

He started toward the front door just as Garrison stepped inside, phone still pressed against his ear.

Jack felt like a teenager who'd been caught sneaking out the window. Which was ridiculous. He hadn't done anything wrong.

Garrison approached, pointed at the bench seat across from his wife, and lifted his eyebrows. There was something commanding about the man, and he was already suspicious. If Jack took off, Garrison would be more convinced something nefarious was going on.

Jack slid into the seat.

Garrison said, "Right. C-L-O-U-D." A moment passed, and then, "For how long?" He waited, then said, "Sure, I'll hold." He glanced at his wife and pointed at the food. "Get that to go, would you?"

She flagged Bonnie down.

Garrison spoke into the phone. "I'm here." He wandered toward the door and continued his conversation.

As Bonnie boxed the meals and Sam paid the bill, Jack pulled out his cell and dialed Harper. No answer. He texted her. *Where are you? I need to talk to you.* No answer. He set his phone on the table.

He didn't know what was happening or what he was expected to do. He wanted to leave and find Harper, but he also wanted to know what Garrison had learned.

Was that so wrong, to want to know the woman he was falling for?

Harper would think so. Would that even matter? Because if he guessed right, Harper was preparing to leave town right now.

He decided to stay another five minutes and shot up a quick prayer. *Don't let her leave before I get there.*

When Bonnie walked away, Sam asked, "What's Harper like?"

Such a loaded question. Wednesday, he'd have had a thousand good things to say about her. Beautiful, kind, genuine, sweet. And a great caretaker. The way she tended Red, the way she loved that old man she wasn't even related to—that told him so much. Harper had a heart made to love, made to care. Two days before, he'd have sworn she'd go out of her way to save a spider's life. But that was then. Today, all the things he'd believed about her seemed wrong. Because she was an ex-con. A liar. A felon.

And even as he told himself that, he didn't believe it.

"I thought I knew her. But apparently…"

When he didn't finish, Sam said, "People change, you know."

He thought of his sister. She'd been a mess all her life, and as far as he knew, she still was. Because some problems couldn't be fixed, not by people. Some problems went soul-deep. With all his heart, Jack believed God could change his sister. He'd held on to faith that God was working on Angel, even though he'd seen no evidence of it.

But what about Harper? She was open to God. She believed, even if her faith was shallow. Right?

Or had she fooled him completely?

He had no idea, but the longer Garrison talked on the phone, the worse Jack felt about this whole thing. Had it been five minutes yet? "I should go." But he didn't move. Because more than he wanted to go, he wanted to know what Garrison had learned.

"Let's just wait another minute."

"What if it's terrible? What if she's running for her life, and your husband has just told the bad guys—"

"Garrison's not talking to bad guys. He's talking to cops. Probably friends at the FBI. Most cops are good people trying to protect the weak. You can trust them."

Sure. He'd always believed that, but Harper didn't believe it. She couldn't, or she wouldn't be in hiding.

Assuming she was.

Wow, Jack's imagination was out of control.

Garrison started toward them, phone still at his ear. He was an imposing man when he wore that serious expression. He spoke into the phone. "Yeah, I'll get back to you."

That didn't sound good.

Garrison ended the call and slid into the seat beside his wife. He folded his hands on the table and met Jack's eyes. "She's a person of interest in a double homicide."

Jack's heart landed on the tile floor. "She didn't do it."

Garrison's smile was weak. "How can you be so sure?"

Jack looked at Sam, then back at Garrison. "Would you believe Sam capable of murder?"

"Sam's not a convicted felon."

Sam's eyebrows rose while her jaw dropped.

Jack said, "Harper did her time."

"You knew about that." Garrison blew out a long breath and leaned back. He held Jack's gaze, and Jack forced himself not to look away, though he was squirming under the man's scrutiny. Because he had no idea what kind of person Harper was. Because though he'd spent time with her and kissed her and—God help him —fallen for her, this ex-cop knew more about her right now than Jack did.

"I don't know you very well," Garrison said, "but you seem like a sharp enough guy. You really think, after everything you learned and after what I just told you, that Harper is on the up and up?"

"Yes." He made the word strong and sure. "If she did anything wrong—and I don't think she did—then she did it in self-defense."

"The murders weren't self-defense, not according to the detective."

"You don't know her."

"Neither do you," Garrison said. Before Jack could argue, he added, "And ten days doesn't count."

"Look, Garrison, I don't know why you think this is any of your business, but—"

"A person acts strangely around law enforcement, it makes a cop wonder. I had a feeling, and I checked it out."

"You need a new hobby."

"I tried knitting once, but it didn't work. Fat fingers." Garrison lifted his gigantic hands. "My lack of hobbies aside, your girlfriend—"

"She's not my girlfriend. She's my tenant."

"—is wanted for murder."

"Let's keep our voices down." She leaned forward and focused on Jack. "Garrison has good instincts. He had a feeling. Now, he knows, and what's done is done."

Yeah. What Garrison had done was alert every law enforcement agency on the eastern seaboard of Harper's whereabouts. With a previous conviction, would she be treated fairly? "What evidence do they have?"

Garrison looked at his wife, and they had one of those silent conversations only married couples had. The kind that drove single people crazy. He wanted to demand they say what they were thinking, but before he could, Garrison spoke.

"No offense, but it's not really your business," he said. "We need to talk to Harper."

Not *his* business? "It's not *your* business. I'm her friend."

Garrison snatched Jack's cell off the table, stood, and pocketed it. "Where is she now?"

"Give me that back."

"Look, I'm not a cop anymore, okay? But the law's still important to me. Now, you can tell me where she is, or I'll call Chief Thomas and alert him there's a wanted woman in his town. He's a good guy, but he's by-the-book. I had a hunch, and now I'm in it. And we're going to deal with it." Jack glared at the man, but Garrison only smiled. "Forget I asked. I'm sure Bonnie has her address."

"She lives next door to me." Jack rattled off the address.

Sam and Jack stood.

Garrison placed his hand on Sam's shoulder. "I want you to stay here." He looked at Jack. "You stay, too. I'll keep you two in the loop."

Sam ducked out from his hand. "I'm going with you."

Garrison shook his head. "She could be dangerous."

"I'm going," she said. "If I'm there, maybe she'll open up. You'll just scare her to death."

Garrison said, "Well, she's a criminal, so—"

"I'm going," Sam said.

"She's not a criminal." But neither Garrison nor Sam was listening to Jack.

Garrison studied his wife's face, then turned toward the door.

"Stubborn, pig-headed..." Garrison was still muttering as he marched away.

Sam patted Jack's shoulder. "You should come. It'll be easier for her if you're there."

This was all his fault, though. If he hadn't gone to McNeal's, Garrison wouldn't have looked her up. "If he gets her thrown in prison..."

"Garrison will hear her out. Trust me, okay?"

He leaned away from her hand. He still didn't know what was going on, and taking a cop with him to find out wasn't the right course of action.

Harper would never forgive him.

JACK WOULD HAVE CALLED to warn her if Garrison hadn't taken his phone. Which was, of course, why Garrison had taken his phone. So instead of warning her, he bolted out the door and took off in his pickup before Sam had climbed into Garrison's Camry.

Maybe Jack could give her a moment's warning, anyway.

But Garrison caught up with him within minutes. Of course. Because Garrison was a former cop and Jack was just a fix-it guy who'd blown everything out of proportion. Who'd thought it was a good idea to run a background check on a woman he cared about. Then he'd somehow brought in a straight-arrow guy like Garrison Kopp to make everything ten times worse.

He was pretty sure he'd spend the rest of his life regretting the previous few minutes.

When he pulled up to the house, Harper was dragging Red's suitcase to the car.

Part of Jack wished they'd wasted more time, given her a chance to get away. Jack would never have seen her again, but at least she might have remembered him with fondness.

She turned toward him. Her face held curiosity as he parked on the narrow street.

The look shifted to suspicion, then fear, as Garrison pulled in the driveway and parked a foot behind the little VW Jetta.

Jack jumped out of his truck and ran across the spotty grass toward her. "Harper, I'm so sorry."

She glanced at him, said nothing, and focused on the others.

Garrison and Sam stepped out of the car and started toward her.

She looked behind her. Jack couldn't blame her. Garrison was six-four, broad-shouldered, and carried himself like a cop. She had to be terrified.

Sam rushed around the car and approached Harper. "We met at the restaurant, remember?"

Harper just stared.

"I'm Samantha Kopp." She stopped a foot from Harper.

Harper turned to Jack, who'd stopped about five feet from her. "What's going on?"

"I'm so sorry. I tried to call earlier—"

"Harper Cloud?" Garrison stepped beside his wife. "I'm Garrison Kopp, a friend of Jack's."

"Friend's a strong word," Jack said, "all things considered."

Garrison ignored him. "Can we go inside? I'd like to talk to you."

Harper looked at Jack. "What did you do?"

"I didn't do this. I mean, not on purpose. I never meant—"

"If you wouldn't mind," Garrison said.

She left the suitcase beside the car, swiveled, and marched up the steps.

Garrison and Sam followed. Jack came in and closed the door behind him. The living room was empty. He hadn't realized before how Harper and Red had filled the place. Red's newspaper was usually folded on the little table between the sofa and the recliner. There was almost always a glass of Gatorade or a cup of coffee there, too. In the afternoons, there'd be a small bowl of some snack. Cashews, peanuts, those gross little soy nuts. Harper's cell phone often rested on the coffee table alongside a novel with a bookmark sticking out.

All that was gone. Jack continued into the kitchen, where Garrison and Sam pulled out chairs and sat at the table. Harper was leaning against the counter, arms folded, staring at the floor.

"Where's Red?" Jack asked.

She didn't look at him when she said, "I was going to pick him up on the way."

"To where?"

She shrugged.

He stepped closer and reached for her shoulder, but she backed away. "Don't."

"I'm sorry."

She didn't acknowledge the words.

Garrison cleared his throat. "Just for the sake of full disclosure," he said, "you should know I'm a former FBI agent. But I'm not a cop right now, and I'm not here in any official capacity." He paused, but nobody spoke. "You acted strangely at the restaurant when I walked up beside you, and then Jack showed up, and he seemed unduly concerned about telling me anything about you. I got suspicious and looked you up, then made a few phone calls. I learned some things that are really troubling."

Still, Harper said nothing.

"The fact that you're packing up and leaving doesn't look good."

She glared at the man. "Am I under arrest?"

Garrison smiled. "I've never actually done one of those citizen's arrests things. Feels very Barney Fife. Of course, he was a cop, wasn't he?"

He watched Harper, and she stared back. Finally, she said, "I don't know who that is."

"What?" He eyed Sam, then Jack. "Kids these days, am I right?"

When nobody answered, Sam said, "I don't think you're putting her at ease."

"This is some of my best stuff," Garrison said.

Sam chuckled and focused on Harper. "Forgive my husband. He's trying to be funny."

Harper narrowed her eyes. "What do you want?"

Garrison blew out a long breath. "Can you please sit down and tell us what's going on?"

"Do I have a choice?"

He shrugged. "The problem is, I know just enough to cause you a lot of trouble. But your friend here"—he nodded toward Jack, who glared at him—"seems convinced you haven't done anything wrong. So I'm willing to give you the benefit of the doubt."

Very slowly, Harper turned to face Jack. "I think you need to go."

"I have no idea how this happened. I just went to McNeal's to see if you were okay."

"It's not his fault you're wanted," Garrison said.

"Wanted?" Harper yanked out a chair and sat heavily.

Garrison's amusement faded. "In connection with a murder."

CHAPTER THIRTY

All Harper's searching for information had led to nothing. No news about her on the internet. No news about the two murdered men. Yet, in no time at all, this total stranger had found the information she'd sought. And now, she'd be arrested. Maybe she wouldn't go to prison. The police couldn't have any evidence against her. She hadn't done it.

But she hadn't committed the last crime, either. And she'd spent two years behind bars for that.

And that wasn't the worst of it. No, the worst had to do with the man in the doorway and the fact that she'd hoped, deep down, that maybe this time would be different. Maybe this man could be different.

She'd been a fool.

Despite the fact that she'd ordered him out, Jack was still there, eyes pleading. And what did that mean? That he cared about her? Fat chance.

Maybe it was like when a person watched a horror flick and wanted to see how it ended. *Would Harper be led away in handcuffs? Would a judge toss her in prison and throw away the key? Stay tuned...*

"What I found concerned me," the ex-cop, Garrison, continued. "Seems you're wanted in connection with a homicide."

Her hands rose as if on their own, palms out. "I swear, I didn't kill those men. I couldn't... I don't even own a gun."

"If you didn't do it"—the man's words were casual, measured—"then how do you know there was more than one victim? And how do you know they'd been shot? And how do you know they were both men?"

Stupid. She was so stupid.

She should ask for an attorney. This guy wasn't a cop, but still...

"Maybe just start at the beginning," the cop said.

Former cop. No, former FBI agent, who'd introduced himself as Garrison. And brought his wife. Which was weird if they were going to haul her off to jail. Who took his wife for that kind of deed? Pregnant wife, if Harper weren't mistaken.

The woman reached out, settled her hand over Harper's. "I think you're going to have to trust somebody."

"And it should be you two? Why?" And how? How to trust anybody when everybody she'd cared about had betrayed her. Everybody but the old man she'd done all this for.

She'd thought Jack might be the exception.

She should order him out, and this time, make sure he left. Because somehow, he'd gotten these people involved. He acted like it was an accident, but that made no sense at all. So maybe Jack had called them... Except she'd seen these two at the restaurant earlier.

Oh, she had no idea. And she couldn't order Jack out, because when she was in custody, she'd need him to take care of Red for her. So he needed to know what was going on.

Fine. She nodded to the fourth chair.

"You sure?" he asked.

"You wouldn't want to miss the best part."

He sat beside her and reached for her hand. She yanked it back. "Don't touch me."

She didn't miss the hurt in his eyes and didn't feel the least bit sorry.

With her focus on the table in front of her, she let the truth settle. This was *her* fault. Her fault for trusting Derrick. Her fault for believing things could be better. Her fault for running when she should have stayed to face the music.

Except... she still didn't know how she could have turned herself in and protected Red.

Garrison cleared his throat. "You were living in Maryland?"

She took a deep breath and met the man's eyes. He had kind eyes. His wife seemed tenderhearted. She'd always been nice to Harper at the restaurant. Anyway, Harper had no choice. "I was working in Las Vegas and met a guy. Derrick Burns. We started dating, sort of. Talking on the phone a lot. He lived in Baltimore, but he came out to see me sometimes. I was working at a nursing home, and he asked me to move to Maryland to take care of his grandfather. I had nothing else going on, so I agreed."

"Let's back up a little," Garrison said. "You were in prison, right?"

Heat filled her cheeks. She didn't want to look at Jack, but as if his presence were magnetized, she glanced his way. That wasn't shock on his face. So he'd already known.

"Years ago, my boyfriend and his friend robbed a liquor store. Emmitt, my boyfriend, was carrying a gun. The owner of the liquor store reached for a shotgun, and Emmitt shot him. Killed him. I was driving the car."

"But you turned yourself in the next day," Garrison said.

She asked, "How did you—?"

"Talked to the detective who arrested you. He said you didn't know about the robbery."

"I didn't. I had no idea. When I saw the news the next day, I realized what had happened. I went to the police and told them the truth. But I wasn't smart enough to get a lawyer, and I believed them when they told me I wouldn't be charged if I told them everything. They arrested Emmitt and Barry, and we all went to prison."

"You just went for two years," Garrison said.

"Which is still ridiculous." Jack's words were vehement. "She didn't do anything."

Garrison glanced at him and nodded. "I agree. The detective does, too. The ADA was trying to make a name for himself, and"—he focused on Harper—"you didn't have a good lawyer to protect you. You got railroaded."

Yes. She closed her eyes, thanked God this guy believed her.

Maybe God had brought her somebody who could help.

Maybe God really did love her. Even her. Even after everything.

"You got out," Garrison prompted, "and then met Derrick and moved to Baltimore."

"Not Baltimore, but Maryland, yes. I wasn't going to, but I had this stalker back in Vegas. I think. I wasn't sure, but then one night..." Her words trailed off. "None of that matters. The point is, I took Derrick's offer because it was a better offer than anything else an ex-con could get, and I was afraid. Probably just paranoid." She scoffed and shook her head. "I thought I'd be safer in Maryland."

"Go on," Garrison said.

"I moved in the spring. Stayed with Red." The thought of him had her glancing at her watch. She looked at Jack. "He needs to be picked up by three."

Jack reached into his pockets, then glared at Garrison. "Can I have my phone?"

"Right." Garrison pulled it from his pocket and handed it over.

What was that about?

As if he'd read her mind, Jack said, "He didn't want me warning you." He offered a half smile, then stepped into the living room and dialed.

She listened while he spoke to someone. She kept her gaze on the table. Garrison and Sam didn't say anything. The kitchen was thick with tension, but nobody tried to cut it.

A moment later, Jack stepped back in. "Steve's daughter is going to take them both back to her house. He'll be fine."

"Thank you." Harper focused on Garrison again. "Derrick, my newer ex-boyfriend, is a gambling addict. Because I have terrible taste in men." She resisted the urge to glance at Jack. "I didn't know about the addiction. If I had, I would never have gotten involved with him. I found out this summer that he owes a lot of money. We were at a party, and a guy who was there, Keith Williams..."

She waited for a reaction from Garrison to the name, but his face was unreadable.

"Anyway, Keith was leaning on Derrick pretty hard. I didn't know what about—I just saw them arguing. But later, Derrick told me Keith was working for his loan shark."

Garrison nodded. Jack started to speak, but Garrison shut him down with a look.

"A week later," she continued, "I overheard Derrick trying to swindle Red out of money. He was asking for two hundred thousand dollars. Red saw right through him and refused."

"Good for him," Jack said.

Neither Garrison nor Sam responded.

"We didn't see Derrick again. He kept his distance, and he and I only talked when I had something to tell him about his grandfather. A month or so ago, Red started really going downhill. Forgetting things, getting angry. Then, it got worse. Headaches, throwing up. Almost as if he'd been drinking. He doesn't drink, so it wasn't that. I called the doctor, and they said it sounded like a virus. I was willing to accept that, but the slurred words, the swaying... I started to fear he'd had a stroke, but nothing else indicated that. I went to get him a fresh bottle of Gatorade one afternoon, and I realized the top had already been opened. I stored them in the garage, and I knew Red wouldn't have gone out there and opened them. I started to get suspicious."

Jack said, "But what does this have to do—?"

"Let her finish." Garrison nodded to her.

She forced a fortifying breath. "I didn't know what it meant, but at that moment, I was more worried about Red than anything else. I decided to run to the grocery store real quick and get him more Gatorade, because he balks if he has to drink anything else, and he needed to stay hydrated. I went to the store." Her voice started to shake with the memories. She wiped sweaty hands on her jeans. "When I got back to my car…" She swallowed. The fear had her voice rising. She couldn't stop the emotions. She couldn't stop the trembling as she remembered that moment.

Jack took her hand, and she met his eyes. She saw kindness there. Tenderness. Trust.

Maybe.

Maybe not.

She held on anyway. "There were two men. One was behind me, so I didn't see him. He held me still. The other wore a mask. He had a knife." She rubbed the healed cut on her neck automatically. "They hurt me." Tears streamed from her eyes as she related the incident. Somehow, she found herself leaning into Jack. His hand gripped her shoulder, her cheek pressed to his chest. She inhaled his rugged scent. If only… But the thought died when Garrison spoke.

"You're saying they walked away?"

She pushed away from Jack and sat up straight. Sam pulled a tissue from her purse, which Harper grabbed to wipe her eyes. "They loaded the Gatorade in the trunk and then walked away."

"Did you call the police?" Garrison asked.

She shook her head. "I had to get back to Red. I'd been gone too long, and he was so sick. What were the police going to do? I didn't see the men's faces. I didn't know what kind of car they drove. I had no information, no evidence."

"A cut on your neck, bruises all over your body." Garrison's eyebrows rose. "Seems evidence enough."

"If I'd known… I didn't know what was going to happen. I didn't see the point. I just had to get back to Red."

The kindness she'd seen in Garrison's face morphed to suspicion. "The point would have been to find the guys who'd beaten you up."

She glared at the man. "I'm a felon. An ex-con. Why would the cops care?"

His suspicion didn't fade a bit. "So you just walked away? That was it?"

"I hid the bruises and took care of Red. I did my job. At that moment, I was more worried about him than anything. I called Derrick, and he came up. I told him what happened and the message they'd given me for him."

"'Tell him we stopped by,'" Garrison clarified from the story she'd just told.

"Right."

"And then what happened?"

"Derrick left. I got Red to bed and took a shower. When I got out, I heard something."

Garrison said, "Define 'something.'"

"It sounded like a door closing. So I went to investigate. And I found..." She swallowed the bile in her throat. "I found two men dead on the floor in the living room."

Garrison sat up straighter. "Just like that? They were there?"

She nodded, unsure what to say next.

"How'd they die?" Garrison asked.

"They'd been shot."

"The old man was in bed?"

"No. He'd heard the noise. He was standing there, staring at them."

Garrison tilted his head to the side. "You don't think he—"

"Absolutely not. There was no gun. And he might've been able to get off one round, but how would he have shot them both? And anyway, there was no blood on the floor. They hadn't been shot there. They'd been left there."

"Why would somebody do that?" Garrison asked.

"To frame me. I mean, that's the only thing that makes sense."

"But why?"

"I don't know. I don't know anything!" She stopped, forced a few deep breaths. Her voice was hysterical, and the higher the pitch, the less credible she sounded.

Jack pulled Harper's hand into his again. Sam patted her shoulder.

"So you left them there?" Garrison's eyebrows were hiked to his hairline.

"After I got Red in the car, I found a payphone and called 911 and told them that I'd seen a disturbance. I called as if I were a neighbor. I left the back door unlocked so the police could get in and find the bodies. I mean, one of the guys was Keith. I'd met him." She swiped at the tears, tried to speak calmly. "I was friends with his wife. Kitty. They have children. I couldn't believe he'd hurt me."

"Wait." Garrison held up his hand, looked toward the ceiling as if he were trying to solve a puzzle, then focused on her again. "How do you know these were the men who assaulted you? You said they'd worn masks."

"I recognized the one's clothes. Not Keith—he'd been the one holding me. I mean, I assume it was him. Oh, and when the guy cut me, he wiped my blood on his jeans. There was a bloodstain there."

Garrison huffed out a short breath. "So the DNA will lead to you."

"I assumed that was the evidence they had against me."

"Doubt it," Garrison said. "Most states' labs are behind. It usually takes months to get DNA evidence back. Must be something else."

"You don't know what, though?"

He shook his head. "All I know is that you're wanted for questioning." Garrison pressed his lips together. "So you were in the house. You found two bodies on the floor. Then what did you do?"

"Red was out of his mind. I didn't think he'd remember any of it, but I had to take care of him. I had to protect him."

"What made you think he was in danger?"

"Oh." She hadn't told them that part. "When I was in the shower, I thought about the Gatorade bottles. I'd bought a case, and they'd come wrapped in plastic. It didn't make sense that they'd been opened before I got them home. Which meant somebody had tampered with them."

Garrison's eyes narrowed. "Go on."

"I think Derrick was trying to kill him."

"Oh, God." Jack breathed the words like a plea, a prayer. "His own grandson?"

"Who else?" Harper turned to face him. "Derrick was desperate for money. Red wouldn't give him any. But when Red dies, he stands to inherit everything. It would have solved all of Derrick's problems."

"But murder?" Jack said. "That's pretty extreme."

She thought about how, way back in Vegas, Emmitt had tried to pin the liquor store owner's death on Barry. How he'd sworn Barry had pulled the trigger. And Barry had sworn Emmitt had done it. Best friends, turned against each other. And since she'd turned him in, Emmitt had turned against her. "Desperate men do desperate things."

"So you took him to the hospital?" By the look on Garrison's face, he already knew the answer to that.

"I couldn't. I was afraid."

"Afraid you'd get arrested," Garrison said. "Afraid you'd go back to prison."

"Yes. No!" She pushed back in her chair and stood. "Not afraid for me. Afraid because nobody would have believed me. I'd have been thrown in jail, and Red would have been turned over to the man who'd tried to kill him."

"But if you had the Gatorade bottles—"

She paced across the kitchen floor. "I didn't realize until after my shower that Red was being poisoned. I'd called Derrick before that. Because I'd been in so much pain after the attack, I'd asked him to get the Gatorade from the trunk for me. So he had to have known I'd figured something out. When I went to grab one of the opened bottles in the garage, they were gone."

Garrison blew out a long breath and ran his hand over his cropped haircut. "Okay. Fine. So there was no evidence. You were scared. You didn't think you could go to the hospital. Except he'd been poisoned. So I guess, what, you just hoped for the best?"

"I'm a nurse, remember? Maybe I'll never be a registered nurse like I wanted, but I understand medical things. I figured out that Derrick had poisoned him with antifreeze." She met Garrison's eyes. "The poor man's antidote is liquor. It's not pretty, but it works."

Garrison's eyebrows hiked again. "So you plied an old man with alcohol to"—he made air quotes with his fingers—"help him."

"Why don't you give her a break," Jack said.

Garrison ignored him. "Where did you go?"

"To a hotel in Newark."

"Harper." Garrison managed to fill the word with incredulity. "Come on. You're missing a step."

"I swear. That's all that happened. And then we came here."

"You need to tell me everything," Garrison said.

"It sounds like she did." Jack stood and wrapped his arm around her back, but she stepped away. She couldn't get close to him or anybody, not right now, not while she fought irritation and fear and the itch to bolt out the back door.

Garrison didn't believe her. She could see the suspicion in his eyes. She took another step away and glanced at the door.

As if he'd read her mind, Garrison stood and walked, calmly, to stand between her and freedom. "What did you do with the bodies, Harper?"

CHAPTER THIRTY-ONE

Jack watched her face. The way her eyes narrowed, the way her mouth formed a little O. The way her skin paled until she looked almost sick. Her blue eyes stood out in bright contrast, rimmed in red. Her hands—her whole body—shook.

Garrison's question hung in the air like the scent of burned dinner.

"I didn't do anything with the bodies." Harper's voice was a whisper. "I left them there."

"I can understand what happened." Garrison's tone was placating, but Jack wasn't buying it. He hoped Harper wasn't either. "You panicked. You had to hide them."

"I swear, I didn't—"

"I just can't figure out how you got them in the car. Did someone help you? Did Red—?"

"He's an old man, Garrison." Jack's voice was too loud. He tried to tamp down his anger. "He uses a walker. And he was sick. Red couldn't possibly have helped anybody move bodies."

"Someone else, then." Garrison stepped forward.

Sam stood and laid a hand on her husband's arm. "Don't jump to conclusions."

Garrison ignored his wife, kept watching Harper.

"I swear," Harper said, "I didn't do anything with them. I... I... I left them right there. I called..." She swallowed, glanced at Jack. "I called 911. I reported a disturbance at the house. Like I told you before. You can check that, right?"

Jack would do anything right now to get her out of this mess. Anything. If only he could figure out how. But even if he could keep Garrison from following if she bolted out the door, Jack wouldn't be able to hold him off long enough for her to get away. If she did disappear into the woods, eventually she'd be found.

She was trapped.

"Call," she said. "Find out if a call came in, if anybody went out to the house."

"I can check, Harper," Garrison said, "but there's no reason to, because the bodies weren't found at the house. They were found stuffed in the trunk of a Cadillac in a parking garage in a little town off I-70."

"No." Her head shook violently. "No, that makes no sense. I left them in the living room." She looked at Jack. "I didn't touch them. How could I touch them?" Her eyes filled with tears and terror. He wrapped an arm around her, and this time, she didn't push him away.

Jack glared at Garrison over her head. "How do you think this tiny woman moved two grown men, two dead bodies, into a car?"

"An accomplice, I assume," Garrison said.

She sobbed into Jack's chest. He held her tighter. Held her for all he was worth. Because she was the victim here. Everything she'd said convinced him of that. How could Garrison not see it?

"This is ridiculous," Jack said. "Where would she have gotten a Cadillac?"

At that, Harper sniffed and turned to Garrison. "Red's car, right?" She looked at Jack. "It was Red's car. I left it... It was in the garage when I left."

"I'm sorry, but the story doesn't work," Garrison said. "Who would leave two bodies in the house for you to find, then remove them after you left?"

"I don't know! I don't..." She took a deep breath, then another. She swallowed, stepped away, and focused on Jack. "You have to take care of Red for me. Don't let Derrick get his hands on him. Derrick can't be trusted."

"It's going to be okay," Jack said, though he had no idea how.

"No. It's not." Her gaze darted around the room—Garrison, Sam, Jack. Her eyes were wide, her lower lip trembling. "It's not going to be okay."

Garrison said, "Harper, why don't you—?"

"Promise me." She held Jack's gaze. "Whatever happens, promise me you won't let Derrick have Red. He'll kill him. If you care about him at all, if you ever cared about me—"

"I never meant..." He stepped toward her, but she backed up, bumped into the counter.

"Don't. Just, please... Red doesn't know anything. He doesn't remember the bodies. He doesn't know about the antifreeze. I didn't want to hurt him."

Jack wanted to reach for her, but everything in her stance told him not to. So he nodded. "I'll take care of him. And I'll get you a good lawyer—"

"That's enough." Garrison's raised voice had them both turning to face him. "Sit down. Both of you. Now." He looked at his wife. "You, too."

Sam's eyebrows hiked, but she slid back into her seat.

After Harper perched on the edge of her chair, Jack sat beside her.

Garrison remained standing. He took a deep breath and ran his hand over his head. "Okay." But then he said nothing else.

Jack rested his hand palm-up on the table between him and Harper. She glanced at it. Then slid her hand into it. He lifted it to his lips and kissed her knuckles.

Tears slid down her cheeks. Her mouth was pinched at the corners, her lips white and pressed together.

This was too much. He still didn't understand any of it. Garrison seemed to be wrestling, too.

"Let's say you're telling the truth," Garrison said.

Harper wiped her tears. "I swear, I would never—"

He held up his hand to silence her. "I'm not saying I believe you. I'm just throwing it out there as a possibility. Maybe Derrick did it."

She sniffed. "That's what I thought at first, because he was the only one who knew about the attack. And maybe he was trying to frame me, to discredit me, in case I told anybody about the poison."

Garrison's eyes narrowed. "You thought that *at first*? What changed?"

"I just can't imagine it. I keep seeing it in my head, and I can't..."

"He's the nicest guy," Garrison said. "Kept to himself."

"Said the neighbors of every serial killer ever," Jack supplied.

"I know." Her eyes squeezed closed, unable to face the obvious truth. "I couldn't imagine Emmitt killing anybody, either. But he did."

Sam, who'd been nearly silent for the entire conversation, tapped on the table. "What I don't understand is why somebody would break in, leave the bodies, and then take them after you left. That doesn't make sense."

"I agree," Garrison said. "If Derrick did it, and if he was trying to frame you, why not leave the bodies there?"

"But that doesn't make sense, either," Jack said. "If he were trying to frame her, leaving two bodies in her living room doesn't work. I mean"—he focused on Harper—"they weren't shot there, right? That's what you said."

"There was no blood on the floor. And I would have heard gunshots."

Garrison paced, seemed to be talking to himself. "If somebody wanted to frame you... We're assuming the bodies were found in the old man's car. But why would they...?"

Jack waited for Garrison to explain what he'd just said. Instead, the other man paced and muttered incoherently. Then, he froze and faced Harper. "You're saying Red owned a Caddy, right?" When she nodded, he considered that. "The Cadillac at the airport had no plates, and the VIN numbers had been filed off. So whoever left it didn't want it traced back to you or Red."

"If they're trying to frame her, then why do that?" Jack asked.

"My first thought"—Garrison focused on Harper—"is that somebody did it to protect you. Or *you* did it to protect you."

"I swear—"

"I heard your story," Garrison said. "I'm not saying I believe it. I'm just trying to work it out. It doesn't make sense."

The four of them were silent. Jack tried to fit all the details he'd heard in the last hour into the larger puzzle. There was a big piece missing. He didn't know what it was, and a glance at Harper's confused expression told him she didn't either.

Nothing had been solved. But Jack was convinced of one thing. Harper wasn't a murderer. She was a sweet, caring, innocent woman trying to protect an old man who was no relation to her, but whom she loved.

He'd stand by her forever. No matter what happened next.

CHAPTER THIRTY-TWO

D errick shifted on his rental car's cheap fabric seats and glanced at the giant fountain soda he'd picked up at the corner store. His throat was parched, but he needed to empty his bladder, and he dared not leave this spot. The rear entrance to the building where Gramps had called from the previous day was quiet right now. Derrick had seen people coming and going from the back—the main door on the side hadn't opened —since he'd arrived that morning. Lots of elderly people, a few younger ones. Based on the sign in front of the building, this was a food bank, but it was only open on Wednesdays. Seemed the rec center Gramps had told him about was open daily.

If Gramps was in there, Derrick hadn't been here in time to see him arrive. He'd come by the night before, but the building had been deserted. So he'd rented a hotel room in Manchester, over-slept, and gotten here by eleven. He'd been watching the building ever since. What if Gramps wasn't here? What if he'd told Harper they'd talked? The two of them could be miles away by now.

Impatience had him tapping the steering wheel. He'd parked behind an adjacent building, where he could see both the side and the rear door through a chain-link fence that separated the two parking lots. He'd keep watching until Gramps came out or someone locked those doors. He had no other leads.

What would he do if they'd run again? He'd have to go into hiding himself. Which meant he'd lose his job, his car, his condo. Without Gramps's money, there was no way Derrick could pay Quentin what he owed him. He'd lose everything. His life, his future.

No.

The very thought had his blood simmering. Gramps had money to spare. Gramps would give it to him, one way or another. He couldn't lose everything he'd worked for. He wouldn't.

Now, it was nearing two o'clock, and activity picked up. Cars came. People went inside. They returned with old folks, climbed into their cars, and left. Three cars, four cars. No sign of Gramps.

A red sedan parked beside the back door, and a middle-aged blond woman went inside. A few minutes later, she came back with two old men, one of whom was leaning heavily on a walker. Was that...? Derrick leaned forward for a better look.

It was Gramps.

Where was Harper, though? Who were these people?

Gramps climbed into the backseat, the other man sat in front, and the woman drove away.

Derrick followed.

Ten minutes later, the car pulled into a driveway in front of a two-story Colonial-style house surrounded by trees. Derrick continued on the road, parked fifty yards or so beyond the driveway, and hurried back. He watched as Gramps hobbled to the door, then slowly made his way up the steps and into the house.

Was this where they'd been staying?

Where was Harper?

The woman came out of the house a few minutes later and drove away.

Derrick jogged back to his car, pulled on his jacket and gloves, then locked the doors. He was emptying his bladder in the woods outside the house when he heard what sounded like a screen door slam. Were they out back?

He crept among the trees, thankful for the dark color of his jacket and jeans, and made it to the backyard. Sure enough, he spied Gramps and the other man sitting in a glass-enclosed sunroom that had been added to the back of the house. They sipped drinks and munched on something while they talked. He could hear them through the glass, though the words themselves were lost. Otherwise, the sunny afternoon was quiet. The leaves rustled in a slight breeze. The birds twittered in the trees.

Derrick was chilled to the bone by the time the other old man went inside the sliding doors. After a few minutes, Derrick darted from the woods to the side of the house to get a closer look. He peered around the corner and into the sunroom. Gramps was sound asleep in a recliner.

The other man was nowhere to be seen.

This was his chance. Nobody knew he was in New Hampshire. Nobody'd seen him in Nutfield. He could creep inside, suffocate the old man, and be gone before anybody saw his face.

He only regretted that when he did this, he wouldn't get his hands on Harper. But killing Gramps would hurt her dearly.

It wasn't the solution he'd hoped for, but for now, it would have to be enough repayment for all the ways she'd hurt him.

He crept to the door. The knob turned, and the door opened silently.

Gramps was snoring softly. Beside him, there was a small, rickety table that held a lamp, a bowl of small orange crackers, and a glass of water.

The sound of a TV drifted from inside the house. Derrick peered through the slider that led to the kitchen. The room was empty.

The other man must've gone in to watch TV when Gramps drifted off. He was probably sleeping, too.

Derrick could do this. He had to do this.

He grabbed a throw pillow covered with bright yellow flowers from an adjacent sofa and stood over his grandfather.

The old man looked good. Healthy, even. Peaceful.

Derrick closed his eyes, took a deep breath. He thought of Quentin and Keith and broken knees and popped-out eyeballs and losing everything.

He opened his eyes and squeezed the pillow in his fists.

Gramps's eyes opened. "Derrick?"

He jumped at the single word. "Hey, Gramps."

The old man blinked. "What are you...? Did Harper tell you where to find me?"

Derrick glanced into the house. No sign of the other guy.

"Nope. She wouldn't have, either. She was hiding from me."

Gramps tilted his head to the side. "From you? Why?"

"You should have given me the money."

Gramps's eyes widened, and his jaw fell.

Derrick pressed the pillow over his face.

Tears streamed from Derrick's eyes as Gramps gripped his wrists, tried to push him off.

He wanted to stop. He wanted to run away. How could he kill this man who'd loved him, who'd protected him after Mom and Dad died? How had Derrick fallen this far?

This was crazy. He wasn't a killer. If he ran now, Gramps might think it had all been a dream. A weird, crazy dream. He hesitated. Let up on the pressure just a tad.

No. He had to do this.

Gramps's arms flailed wildly, and he knocked over the lamp.

The crash reverberated in the room.

A shout came from the house. "Red?"

Derrick dropped the pillow, met Gramp's wide, terrified eyes.

And bolted.

CHAPTER THIRTY-THREE

Harper sat as still as she could and watched Garrison, who was still standing and staring at nothing.

The silence would kill her. Not Derrick, not prison. Waiting while Garrison processed all she'd told him—that would be the death of her.

Jack squeezed her hand and offered a slight smile. Part of her wanted to hate him for getting these people involved. But another part of her was glad he had. Because now, whatever happened, at least the running was over. She could tell her side of the story. As long as Gramps was safe, she could take whatever was coming.

What laws had she broken?

She hadn't stolen anything or hurt anyone. Red was an adult, and he'd come with her willingly. All along, she'd tried to do the right thing. For her sake. For Red's sake.

But would anybody believe her?

Harper glanced at Sam, who gave her a slight smile as if this were a perfectly normal situation.

Garrison stared beyond her.

Jack pushed back in his chair. "Look—"

"Just let me think," Garrison said.

Jack met her eyes, shrugged.

"Honey," Sam said, "do you think you could let us know what you're thinking?"

He blew out a long breath and met Harper's eyes. "Your story is strange. If I'd heard it from anyone else, I'd have dismissed it out of hand because it doesn't make sense."

Harper couldn't seem to form words, but Jack said, "You said 'if.' Does that mean you believe her?"

"I do," Garrison said. "I'm good at telling if people are lying, and I don't think you are."

"I'm not," she said. "I swear I'm not."

Garrison's mouth flattened into a smirk. "And I hope that if you'd made up a story, it would've been a little better than what you've told me. Made-up stories make sense. Usually."

Harper swallowed, nodded.

"None of that changes the fact that you're wanted in connection with two murders. You need to turn yourself in."

She stared at the table. She could do that, but what would she do with Red? Would he go with her back to Maryland? Could she have Roger hire him another nurse while she dealt with this? Would anybody be able to protect him from Derrick? Would anybody believe he was trying to kill his grandfather?

"I'll call the detectives investigating the murders," Garrison said. "I'll give them a heads-up, tell them you're here and you had no idea you were wanted. I'll try to pave the way, but I can't promise anything."

"I didn't do it."

Garrison held her gaze. "I believe you." He stood, grabbed his cell phone, and went out the front door.

"I didn't get them involved on purpose," Jack said. "It's important to me that you understand that. I was worried. It all just got out of hand."

"That's the truth." Sam's voice was kind. "My husband can be like a dog with a bone sometimes. He got suspicious. He misses being a cop."

Harper just shrugged.

"I think," Jack continued, "maybe this is better than you running away again. Maybe it's better if you deal with it."

Jack was probably right.

"I believe you, too," Sam said. "And I'll be praying. God can handle this." Her smile was kind, gentle. "Do you mind if I use your restroom?"

"Help yourself."

After Sam walked away, Jack squeezed Harper's hand. "I never doubted you for a minute."

Right. She looked at him, raised her eyebrows.

"I was afraid you were in trouble," he said. "I never thought…" He swallowed, glanced away, then met her eyes. "Okay, I doubted you, a little. Can you forgive me?"

Had he done anything wrong? "I've lied to you about everything, and I was about to take off without a word."

"None of it was my business."

"Maybe," Harper said. "What's going to happen now?"

"I have no idea. I don't know Garrison well enough to guess, and the guy's sort of an enigma. Scary intimidating cop who tells stupid dad jokes."

Harper nearly smiled. "My dad tells stupid dad jokes, too."

"They all do. I probably will someday, too. If I'm ever lucky enough to…" He turned his chair toward Harper, then turned her chair so they were facing each other. He took her hands and met her eyes. "I'm with you in this. Whatever happens now, whatever you need me to do. I'm on your side. I'll make sure Red is taken care of, protected from Derrick. I'll do whatever you need me to do."

A flood of emotions filled her, almost too big to name. His kindness, his quick understanding, his generosity. How could she refuse him anything?

How could she draw him into her nightmare?

"Don't." His voice was intense, and he leaned closer. "You're so easy to read. Don't push me away. Not now. Please."

"Maybe after I get this all—"

"No. Not after. Circumstances are never going to be perfect, Harper."

"But none of this is your problem."

"It is, though. It is my problem, because it's your problem. And I care for you."

She leaned away, wanted to stand, to put distance between them so she could think. "You don't even know me."

"I know you risked your own life and freedom to protect an old man who's not even related to you. I know you've been through hell, and all along, you've just been trying to take care of him. No thought for your own comfort, your own needs."

"You make me sound so noble."

"Noble." He nodded. "That's the right word."

She looked away. "It's not. You don't know."

And even if he did, even if he really did care about her, could she trust him?

"I want to be here for you."

Harper pushed back her chair and stood.

Jack stood, too. Her plan to get farther from him so she could think was not working. Because there he was, tall, broad, beautiful, and just inches away.

Sam stepped out of the bathroom. Surely Jack would back up now, put more space between them. But he didn't move.

Sam disappeared into the living room. A moment later, the front door opened and closed.

They were alone.

"I'm not..." She swallowed, shook her head. Tried to think. "I can't be who you want me to be. I don't know you. I don't trust... easily."

"I've given you plenty of reasons not to trust me."

No, that wasn't true. "You've been nothing but kind to me. And you didn't have any reason to trust me."

"I've seen how you've taken care of Red. How you've been breaking your back to provide for a man who, by all accounts, is very wealthy. How devoted you are to him. I was afraid for you. I certainly didn't intend for this to happen."

None of that changed the truth, though. Of course Jack wasn't trying to hurt her, not yet. But her history was too long to be discarded that easily. "Every man who's ever found me attractive has lied to me, hurt me, treated me like..." But she couldn't finish the sentence. Because the men in her past had treated her exactly the way she'd acted. She'd never deserved better because she'd never behaved better.

She didn't know if she could now.

And she didn't want to reduce either one of them to the kinds of relationships that littered her past.

"Not all guys are like the yahoos you've fallen for," he said. "Is your father like that?"

Her father had his issues, but he was a good man. He'd treated her mother with respect. "No."

"How about Red. Is he like that?"

"Of course not." She thought of the men from her past. Then all the men at the strip club, men with handfuls of dollar bills and opened mouths and lust in their eyes. "Because of how I look, men don't see me, the real me. They want things from me because I'm..." She didn't know how to finish that statement.

"Beautiful?"

Her cheeks warmed, and she didn't respond.

His eyes crinkled at the corner. "Well, then, you can trust me. Because I think you're a dog."

The way he was looking at her belied his words. Every cell in her body responded to him. It was as if her entire being were leaning toward him, needing him.

He lowered his gaze to her lips. "Woof, woof."

She shouldn't kiss him again. If she did, she'd fall for him completely. And then she'd be lost.

But maybe Jack really was different. Maybe this was a man she could trust.

Anyway, she didn't have the strength to resist.

His lips brushed hers. He paused and waited for her to step back. Which she probably should have. But she'd lost all control when it came to Jack Rossi.

She leaned in, kissed him back, and surrendered her heart.

CHAPTER THIRTY-FOUR

J ack's cell phone rang, and Harper jumped as if they'd been caught doing something wrong. But kissing Harper wasn't wrong. Nothing had ever felt so right.

Though she leaned away, he didn't release her. He wanted to ignore the call, to ignore the outside world and stay locked in an embrace with Harper forever.

But the moment was over.

"You should get that," Harper said.

He reluctantly pulled his cell from his pocket. "Hello?"

"Jack? It's Elizabeth."

Oh, no. "Is Red okay?"

"I don't know. Dad called, said he thinks maybe he had a heart attack, but he wasn't sure. Just said he was clutching his chest and talking gibberish. Dad called 911."

Jack met Harper's eyes. "What hospital?"

He got the details and hung up.

Harper's face was white as death. "Please tell me he's all right."

"They're not sure what happened, but to be on the safe side, they took him to the hospital." Not exactly what Elizabeth had said, but it would keep Harper from panicking. He took her hand and headed for the front door. She snatched her purse from the counter on the way. Harper started for her car but pulled up when she saw Garrison's car parked right behind hers.

Jack said, "I'll drive."

Sam was seated in Garrison's Camry. Garrison was on the phone, pacing in the yard. He saw them, then spoke into the phone. "Hold on a sec." He covered the phone and met Jack's eyes. "What's up?"

"We have to go." Harper's words were frantic, terrified.

"Red's on his way to the hospital," Jack said.

Garrison headed toward his car. "We'll follow you."

Harper stared forward silently throughout the drive to Manchester. Jack tried to engage her in conversation a couple of times, but she barely seemed to register his words. Finally, Jack parked at the doors to the ER, and Harper rushed inside.

Jack parked and hurried to meet her. Harper was nowhere to be seen. He approached the nurse behind the desk. "My friend just came in looking for Harold Burns."

"She's back there with him. You'll need to take a seat."

He started to argue, but the woman cut him off. "Are you family?"

He blew out a long breath. "Just a friend."

"Then have a seat."

He turned, surveyed the room, and saw Steve in a chair on the far side. He crossed to him and sat. "What happened?"

Steve shook his head. "He fell asleep in the sunroom while we were talking, so I went inside to watch TV." He lifted his trembling hand to rub his nose. "I mighta drifted off myself. I heard a crash. I got up, and when I got into the sunroom, Red was in the chair. His skin was gray. His eyes were terrified. And he was talking about someone trying to kill him."

Jack had witnessed that fear in the old man's eyes when he had one of his dementia moments. "What did he say?"

"Something about someone named Derrick. Said he was trying to smother him."

Jack's stomach dropped. He looked around the emergency

room, but Derrick could be anywhere. Jack had no idea what the man looked like.

"Don't know who Derrick is," Steve said. "Figured he was doing like he did that day at the rec center. But the color of his skin, the way he was clutching his chest... I called an ambulance."

"You did the right thing," Jack said.

"Yeah." Steve nodded, then shook his head. "You know what's weird, though?" He paused, seemed to be thinking back. "Elizabeth put these throw pillows on the couch out there. Nobody ever touches them. And the sofa was a good five feet away from Red. But when I went out there, one of those pillows was on the floor by the back door."

Derrick.

It didn't make sense. And it was the only thing that did make sense. "What caused the crash?"

"The lamp. He must've knocked it over."

Or Derrick had. Or he had been trying to get away from Derrick.

"Be right back." He left Steve in his seat and rushed to meet Garrison as he and Sam walked in. "Derrick's here."

Garrison froze. "What do you mean?"

Quickly, Jack told Garrison everything Steve had said. "Red didn't know his grandson had been trying to kill him. So why would he say that? Derrick must be here."

Garrison stared beyond him at nothing for a moment, then nodded once and turned. He was already dialing his phone by the time he stepped back into the cold November afternoon.

CHAPTER THIRTY-FIVE

Harper sat by Gramp's side in the ER. Now that the truth was out, she could go back to calling him Red, even if she thought of him as family. The door was closed to their little space. Outside the room, the rest of the hospital buzzed with activity. Footsteps, voices, ringing phones. Inside the room, the only sounds came from Red's quiet snoring and the hum of machines monitoring his health. And the smells. After working in a nursing home, the hospital smells shouldn't bother her, but right now, her stomach churned.

It seemed like hours had passed, though it had probably been no more than one. Occasionally, the nurse came in and checked his vitals. Once, she'd drawn blood, probably looking for troponin, the protein in the blood that rises in response to heart damage. So far, nobody'd felt the need to tell Harper any of their findings.

A woman had wheeled in a computer to ask about Red's health insurance and medical history. Now that Harper had been found by the authorities, she could share his insurance information. She'd need to call Red's lawyer and let him know what was going on. And she'd need to stay with Red to make sure Derrick didn't get to him.

She watched the monitors but saw nothing to worry about. His heartbeat was steady. His pulse was normal. His blood pressure was a little high, but nothing to be concerned about.

She took his cold hand and closed her eyes. *Dear God. Please save him. Whatever happens to me, please protect him.* She prayed for his health, for his life. And then she prayed for herself. That God would show her what to do now that her story had fallen apart. That He would protect them both. That the truth would be brought to light, and that she would be free of the charges that were no doubt coming.

And she prayed for Jack. *Lord, You know how I feel about him. Protect him from this mess I've made. Make a way for us to be together. If that's not what You want, then please, help me not to care for him.*

Finally, an Asian woman stepped into the room. She was petite with short black hair and wore a white coat over scrubs. "I am Dr. Pham."

Harper stood and shook her hand. "Harper Cloud."

The woman peeked at Red, who was still sleeping. She lowered her voice. "You are his granddaughter?"

"I'm his caretaker, his nurse. I have legal documentation, if you need to see it."

"Do you have it with you?"

Harper dug into her small purse and pulled out the paperwork. The doctor read it over and handed it back. "The ECG showed that Mr. Burns suffered a minor heart attack." She kept her voice low, and Red didn't stir. "The blood tests confirmed that. Right now, his vitals are steady. Nevertheless, we will keep him here for a few days. He will be transferred to a room, and I will hand over his care to a cardiac specialist."

Harper took all the information in, tried to think of something intelligent to say but came up with nothing. "Thank you so much."

She smiled. "They will take good care of him upstairs." With that, the doctor left, and Harper sat beside him. A few minutes later, his eyes opened.

Harper took his hand. "Hey, sleepyhead. How you feeling?"

He squeezed her hand and looked around the drab room, his eyes settling on the monitors beside him before he focused on her again. "I'm alive, I guess."

She let out a short laugh. "That you are, thank God."

He started to smile, but the look faded. His eyes widened, and he held her hand tighter. "Derrick. He was there."

Uh-oh. He was awake but not as lucid as he'd first seemed. "We're still in New Hampshire. What would Derrick be doing here?"

"He was there. He found me."

"That's imposs—"

"Listen to me."

She quieted at the urgency in his voice.

"I called him yesterday from Steve's phone."

No, no, no. Harper covered her mouth with her palm.

"I showed him where I was with that pin-thing." Red's voice quivered. "He told me how." Tears filled the old man's eyes. "He told me not to tell you. Said he wanted to surprise you." His grip loosened. "I'm just a foolish old man. I believed him."

"It's okay." Harper worked to keep her voice steady, to keep him calm. She glanced at the monitor, saw his heart rate had increased. "It's fine. It's okay that he's here."

Tears filled the old man's eyes as he looked away. "He almost killed me. Put a pillow over my face. Tried to smother me."

She sat heavily in the chair. "I should have... I tried to—"

Red met her gaze. "Tried to what? Did you know he might...?" His voice was filled not with accusation but surprise.

She took his hand. "I didn't want you to know."

"You need to tell me what you're talking about."

"Remember how sick you got those last few days before we left?"

He nodded, eyes narrowed.

"He was poisoning your Gatorade. That's why I made you drink that whole weekend, to get the poison out of your system."

His eyes narrowed. "It was vodka, wasn't it? You kept calling it medicine, but—"

"It's an antidote to ethylene glycol. Antifreeze. Not the best one, certainly not the easiest one. I didn't want to take you to a hospital." She hoped he wouldn't ask why, because after the scare he'd had, the last thing he needed was to be reminded of the bodies in his living room.

"You were trying to protect Derrick. And trying to protect me from knowing the truth."

She nodded and swallowed the half-truth. Mostly she'd been trying to protect herself and Red from whoever had killed those men.

"You took good care of me." He looked away. "My own grandson..."

She didn't know what to say. Didn't know how to soften the blow for this kind, gentle man. "He's just... He's in too deep."

They were silent for a few minutes. His heart rate returned to normal. He kept his gaze away from her when he said, "I guess I should have just given him the money."

"None of this is your fault."

"I'll keep telling myself that."

She squeezed his hand. "Look at me."

Slowly, his head turned toward her. She leaned a little closer. "You've been nothing but good to him. He got himself into a terrible mess, and now he doesn't know how to get out of it."

He stared at the ceiling. "He couldn't go through with it. All of a sudden, I couldn't see. Couldn't breathe. Couldn't fight. I thought I was a goner. And then, he just let up."

"Thank God." At least Derrick had a sliver of decency left in him.

"I was ready to go see my Bebe. I was ready." He met her eyes again. "If anything happens to me, I want you to know, whenever the Lord wants to take me home, I'm ready."

"Don't say—"

"I'm glad, though." He took a breath. "Glad he didn't do it.

Glad he doesn't have to live with that on top of everything else."

"Me, too," Harper said. Not for Derrick's sake. Derrick deserved whatever he got. But she couldn't imagine losing Red. Not now. Not yet. *Please, God, not by murder.*

~

THERE WAS A SOFT KNOCK. Harper waited for a nurse to walk in. When none did, she stood and opened the door. Jack and Garrison stood outside. Jack said, "How is he?"

"Come on in."

She stepped aside, and Jack came into the room, bringing his steady presence with him. "Hey, Red. How you feeling?"

While Red answered, Garrison gripped Harper's arm. "We need to talk."

Jack pulled up a chair. He sent her a quick nod, then focused on Red.

She didn't want to walk away, but they weren't giving her much choice. "Be right back."

Red waved her out, and she followed Garrison down a corridor and into a room not much larger than the exam room she'd just left. It was like a waiting room. Lining the walls were chairs interspersed with a table here and there.

Inside were two men. She recognized them both—regulars at McNeal's. She'd heard one called Chief. The other was the guy with the drawl she'd served her first day at work. They stood when she walked in, straight and solid. Were they going to arrest her right here?

She turned to Garrison. "Please, don't let them—"

"Don't worry," Garrison said. "I'm on your side."

Right. She'd heard that before. The cops in Vegas had told her to trust them, too. She wasn't stupid enough to get herself into the same mess twice. Jack had promised to take care of Red. She'd tell whoever these people were everything, but not alone. "I want a lawyer."

Garrison sighed. "You're not in custody. We're not here to question you or arrest you. We're trying to protect you and Red. We think Derrick is here."

"Oh." The icy backbone she'd pretended melted away, and she collapsed into a chair. "Yes. Red said the same thing."

Garrison stepped inside. "These are friends of mine. Brady Thomas."

The taller and older of the two, the one they called Chief, stepped forward and shook her hand.

"And this is Eric Nolan." The younger one did the same, and then they both sat.

"Brady's the Nutfield Chief of Police, and Eric's a detective."

"You work at McNeal's, right?" the chief asked.

"Uh-huh. You're here because of what Red said?"

Chief Thomas nodded once. "Seems the other older gentleman, Steve, thought Mr. Burns was hallucinating, but based on what we learned from Garrison and your friend"—he glanced at a small notebook—"Jack Rossi, it seems it's possible this Derrick person may have tried to kill his grandfather."

She nodded, swallowed. "Red said he tried to smother him, but then... I guess he couldn't go through with it."

"But he's tried before?" the chief clarified.

"I can't prove it, but he put antifreeze in Red's drinks."

"You should have called the police right away."

She chuckled, though she felt anything but amused. "Things got a little out of hand."

Chief Thomas glanced at Garrison, who said, "That's a long story. It's not relevant to this discussion."

The chief stared at Garrison another moment, then said, "You'll tell me later," and turned back to Harper. "I'll contact the Manchester PD, and I'll have all the surrounding departments on the lookout for Burns. I've already spoken to hospital security, and they have his photo and know to keep an eye out for him."

She glanced at Garrison, then back at this man. These total strangers, these cops, were on her side? They were going to help her protect Red?

She didn't have to do it alone.

Tears welled in her eyes. She tried to blink them back, to hide the emotion that bubbled up inside of her. "Sorry. I'm just... Thank you."

"Just doing my job," the man said.

The other cop, Eric, snatched a couple of tissues from a box on a table, stood, and handed them to her. "Here you go, ma'am."

Ma'am. He almost sounded like home.

She dried her cheeks and reined in her emotions. "Thank you."

"I'm a little curious, though." The chief looked from her to Garrison and back. "Why would you need a lawyer?"

Garrison stood. "Part of that long story."

"Sounds like a story I need to hear now," the chief said.

Garrison just laughed. "Thanks for coming, guys. I'll take it from here." He shuffled the two cops out the door.

After they walked out, Sam walked in. Garrison closed the door while Sam sat beside Harper. "I'm working on putting together a group of people who can sit with Red. I'll help, of course. And Jack suggested Ginny, his real estate—"

"Wait." Harper leaned away. What was she talking about? "That's my job. I don't need help."

Garrison sat on the other side of her. "You have to go to Maryland and get this cleared up."

"What?" She turned to him, tried to figure out what he'd said. "I can't do that. I have to stay. He had a heart attack. He needs me."

"The hospital is keeping him for a couple of days. You can get to Maryland and back before he's released."

"But what if they arrest me? What if they throw me in jail?"

On her other side, Sam took her hand, but Harper snatched it away and stood. She turned to face them. "No. I can't."

A knock sounded, and then Jack stepped in.

She stared at him. Did he know what was going on?

Whose side was he on? She hadn't done anything wrong, but they were all against her.

"Why aren't you with Red?"

"A couple of cops came in to take his statement." He turned to Garrison. "Friends of yours?"

Garrison nodded. "She met them."

"What'd you tell them?" Jack asked.

"Nothing about the murders," Garrison said. "Just about Derrick."

Jack stared at the man a moment, then focused on her. "You okay?"

"He wants me to leave Gramps here and go to Maryland."

Garrison rose, too. They seemed to be in some sort of three-person stand-off. Garrison blew out a breath. "What did you think, that you were just going to be able to pretend it didn't happen? Two men have been murdered, Harper. You have information about those murders. They have evidence—"

"I didn't do anything. What evidence could they have?"

"I don't know," Garrison said. "I do know that as we speak, technicians are combing the Burns house, looking for more."

"Why? How would they—?"

"I called them," he said. "I told them the Cadillac likely belonged to Red Burns."

Panic rose like a tornado in May. "They didn't die at the house!" Her voice was too high, but she couldn't control it. "I didn't do it. I didn't kill anybody."

Jack took her hand. "Until you go and tell them your side of the story—"

"I can't! They won't believe me. They'll throw me in prison. And then Red—"

"He'll be taken care of." The words came from Sam. She stood and walked to Harper's other side. "We'll take care of him until you get back. That's what I started to tell you. Somebody's going to stay with him, either in his room or outside his door, constantly until his grandson is located. And hospital security will be watching out for him."

So Red would be protected. At least for now. And she'd turn herself in. She could already feel the handcuffs. "But what if…?" She looked at Garrison, at Sam. Then she focused on Jack. "What if they don't believe me? What if I don't come back?"

"If the worst happens," he said, "I'll hire you the best attorney money can buy. You didn't do it. They won't convict you."

"But what about when Red gets out of the hospital?"

"I'll take care of him," Jack said. "God forbid you end up in jail, I'll take him back to Maryland. I'll stay with him until you can again. And I'll be close."

"What? You can't—"

"And I'm going with you tonight."

Tonight.

They wanted her to go now.

To face the nightmare she'd left in Maryland.

To tell the police everything.

To trust that this time, this time, the justice system would get it right.

And then, his words registered. "You're coming with me?"

"Of course." He stepped closer, kissed her forehead. "We're in this together."

CHAPTER THIRTY-SIX

Derrick cursed himself again.

Why had he let up? Another thirty seconds, a minute at most, and Gramps would have been dead. There would have been no autopsy for an eighty-five-year-old man with health problems. Nobody would have questioned it.

Derrick could have slipped out the back door, returned to Maryland, and been there to receive the sad news that his grandfather had passed away.

And then he would have inherited everything. He wouldn't have had the money within a week, but knowing the inheritance was coming would have satisfied Quentin.

Now... Now he had no idea what to do. Because now Gramps knew how desperate Derrick was. And Harper had already known. Had they told the police? Were they looking for him?

Derrick had been in his rental in the hospital parking lot for hours. He'd followed the ambulance here. Then, he saw Harper arrive with a man. Was it Jack, the man Gramps had told him about? Were they together now?

The anger rose again. Harper belonged to Derrick. He'd rescued her from that dreary life in Vegas, wiping geriatric butts for a living, working two jobs just to make ends meet. He'd loved her, provided a home for her, given her gifts. He'd tried to be the man she wanted, the man she needed. And she'd betrayed him. And apparently, she'd already moved on.

As if Derrick had never mattered at all.

But he did matter. He did! If Harper didn't see that... Why didn't Harper see that? Why didn't she realize what kind of man Derrick was? How important he was?

Well, if she didn't, who cared? He'd show her. He'd show them all.

He itched to hit a casino, to prove his worth once and for all. To fix this with one hand of cards. He'd do it, too. Except right now, Quentin had no idea where Derrick was. If he set foot in any casino in the country, Quentin would hear about it. And the last thing Derrick needed was to have another run-in with the loan shark and his goons. He had nothing to give them. The cash he'd gotten from Roger was nearly gone, thanks to the wild goose chase he'd been on this week.

So a casino was out. Derrick could run, far and fast. Except Quentin would eventually find him. Derrick knew how Quentin dealt with people who tried to skip out on their debts.

He rubbed his eyes, as he'd done a thousand times since Vegas, to assure himself they were both there.

No, running away wasn't an option. He had to get the money to pay Quentin back. And he only had a couple more days to do it.

Assuming Gramps remembered what happened, would anybody believe him? Nobody had seen Derrick in town, and the dementia sometimes made Gramps say crazy things. Maybe if Harper hadn't figured out about the poison, nobody would believe Gramps now.

Except Harper would believe him. And if she hadn't put two-and-two together about the Gatorade before, she probably would now.

So... Derrick would come up with a plan. He could deny he'd been at the other man's house, deny he'd smothered his grandfather. He could admit to having been in New Hampshire, tell the police he'd come to find his grandfather. That Harper had stolen him away, and he'd been searching. All that was true. And plausible.

He could say he'd gone to the food bank where Gramps had called him from and watched, but the place was deserted by the time he got there. So he'd planned to go back the next day. He'd been watching for them. That made sense, right?

It would be Derrick's word against Gramps's.

Without evidence, nobody could convict him.

But they could arrest him.

He'd seen two men arrive earlier who looked like cops. Their dark sedan was still parked against the curb near the ER doors. They were probably taking statements right this moment.

Derrick had to get out of there.

He had to figure out how to keep tabs on Harper without following her too closely.

He mulled the problem over. Would she stay with the guy in the pickup? Would that eventually lead Derrick to where she lived? Maybe he could duct tape a cell phone to the bottom of the truck, then use an app to track it.

There had to be a cheaper option. He pulled out his cell and searched for ideas. Yes, a GPS tracker that would report their every move, and it was on sale at a store in town. It was a risk to leave here, but surely Gramps wouldn't be released from the hospital anytime soon. Harper would stay by his side. So Derrick should have time.

He backed out of his parking space and drove down the aisle where the pickup had parked, snapping a photo of its license plate, just in case. If the truck was gone when Derrick returned, Tank could track it for him. The private investigator had sworn off helping him, but the man could be persuaded.

He pulled out of the parking lot and headed for the store, where he bought two trackers, just in case he needed one for Harper's car, too, assuming he ever found it. He was back in thirty minutes. The pickup was still there. Derrick parked close to it, downloaded the app he'd need to track the devices. When he had a strong signal, he made sure nobody was watching and duct-taped the tracker to the underside of the pickup. Not exactly the way the instructions had written it up, and if the truck went through puddles, the device would likely be ruined, but he had no other choices right now.

Derrick climbed back into his rental and drove away. At least he had that problem solved. By the time he figured out where Harper was staying, he'd have made a plan.

He could still make this work. He had to get the money out of Gramps. Derrick had failed to kill him, and now Gramps would change his will. Which meant Derrick would have to find a way to compel Gramps to hand over the money.

Gramps wouldn't do it to save Derrick's life. He'd already made that clear. But he'd do anything to save Harper's.

That was Derrick's only hope.

CHAPTER THIRTY-SEVEN

Harper watched as Jack settled her suitcase into the backseat of his pickup and thought about the contents inside. What was the proper attire for surrendering to the police? Should she plan to wear slacks and a nice blouse, try to show them that she was a normal person, a trustworthy professional? Or would that make it look as if she were trying too hard?

Did it matter what she wore? What she said? When she walked into that police station, would they see a twenty-eight-year-old healthcare worker who loved the old man she cared for as if he were her own grandfather? Would they see a woman who'd done everything in her power to protect him?

Or would they see an ex-con who'd run?

She couldn't think about it or she'd melt into a puddle of fear.

Jack's phone rang, and he walked away and answered it.

She and Jack had already been to his house so he could pick up a few things. He'd insisted she stay by his side, just in case Derrick was close. She hadn't argued. Derrick *was* close. As stupid as it would sound if she said it out loud, she knew she was being watched. Eyes on her burned like the Vegas sun. Somebody was watching her. She'd forgotten the way she'd always felt, as if danger lurked around every corner. Back in Vegas, and even in Maryland, it had been so frequent that the anxiety had felt like it was part of her. And then she'd come here to this idyllic little town, and she'd felt safe.

For less than two weeks.

She could hear Jack talking quietly on the phone. Probably making arrangements for this last-minute trip.

She leaned against the side of his truck and inhaled a deep breath. The fresh country air was perfect. Just what she needed. So unlike the stale recycled air in prison.

Harper couldn't go back. She couldn't.

Was she really doing this? Was she really going to walk into a police station and tell them her story? And trust they'd believe her?

They wouldn't. And then she'd end up behind bars. Again. For a crime she hadn't committed. Again.

Her gaze shifted to the forest behind the house. She could run, just take off into the woods.

Right. How long would she last on the run? Hiding from Derrick had been one thing. But hiding from the police and... Garrison was former FBI, so they'd be on her trail. She probably wouldn't last a day. And when they caught her, they'd never believe her story.

Anyway, even if Jack and his friends would take care of Red, Red would never understand why she'd abandoned him.

After what Derrick had done, her leaving might just kill the old man.

She had no choice. She had to go back to Maryland. She had to face whatever was coming and trust that the police would at least listen to her side of the story. This time, she wouldn't go alone. Garrison had already compiled a list of defense attorneys. She'd make calls while Jack drove. An attorney on her side... This time, they'd believe her.

She told herself that, but nausea rose anyway.

Jack hung up the phone and walked toward her. "You okay?"

She crossed her arms against the chill in the air. "I'm ready."

He studied her. "You're white as a sheet."

"I'm scared."

He raised his eyebrows. "Did you kill those men?"

The question threw her. She blurted, "No."

"Were you trying to kill Red?"

"Of course not."

He leaned in and kissed her cheek. "Let's trust the Lord on this one, okay?"

She had no idea how to do that.

Jack added, "Jesus said, 'The truth will set you free.' Do you believe that?"

The truth hadn't set her free before. It had landed her in prison. But... she'd been guilty before. Not of murder, but of plenty of other stuff. She'd been guilty, and she'd served two years. As awful as it had been, prison had changed her. She'd come out determined to live right. She'd emerged sober, wiser about men and all the relationship issues she'd had before. She'd given up her dream of fame and fortune and gotten the job at the nursing home, where her favorite patient had told her about Jesus. Then she'd met Derrick. She'd been fooled at first, but when he'd shown his true colors, she'd ended that relationship. And through Derrick, she'd met Red, who'd told her more about Jesus. She'd believed in her Savior, and she'd been set free from her past because of Him. Prison had been awful, but it had been the beginning of this walk of faith.

"I do believe it," she said. "Maybe I won't be physically free, but He has set me free from my past."

Jack stepped nearer. He took both her hands, looked into her eyes, and smiled. "I believe He means to set you free from all of it, right now. On the other side of this storm, you're going to find peace. And I'm just happy to be along for the ride."

She let out a short laugh that surprised both of them. "You might be a little bit crazy."

"I've been called worse." He wrapped his arms around her.

When his lips touched hers, those worries floated away like vapor. He tasted of confidence and love. How could she not trust this man who'd done so much for her already? Who was willing to go on this journey with her, to keep her safe, to stand by her through all the ugliness that was surely to come.

Maybe Jack was right. Maybe this was the beginning of the end. Maybe, soon, she would be safe.

Maybe this time, the truth really would set her free.

THE END.

BEAUTY IN BATTLE
BOOK 3 IN THE BEAUTY IN FLIGHT SERIES

THE TRUTH IS OUT, but will it set her free or land her in the grave?

Harper doesn't want to return to Maryland to face the police. The mess she left behind makes her look guilty of the worst, but it's too late to run again. Red is safe and the authorities are waiting. At least Jack is by her side.

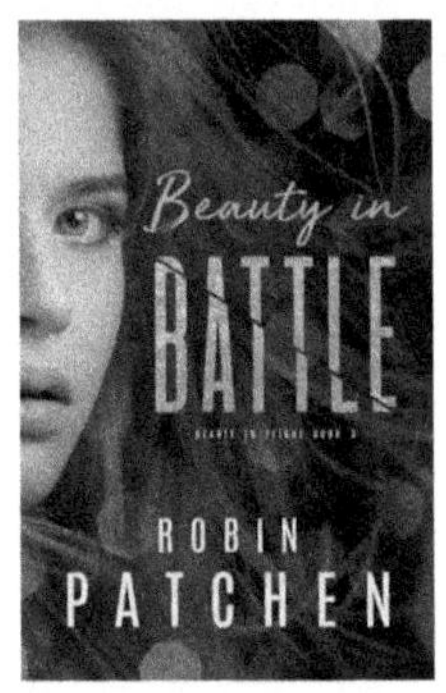

Now that Jack knows the truth, his feelings for Harper are deeper than ever. He's not about to leave her side, especially knowing a killer is after her.

But Derrick is on their trail, and he's come unhinged. And he may not be the biggest threat lurking.

Don't miss the exciting conclusion of the Beauty in Flight series. Buy BEAUTY IN BATTLE today.

ACKNOWLEDGMENTS

No story comes together without help. I owe thanks to my critique partners, Sharon Srock, Terri Weldon, Pegg Thomas, Jericha Kingston, Candice Patterson, Kara Hunt, and Normandie Fischer. You make me look good.

Thank you to my editor, Ray Rhamey, and to Misty Beller for all your marketing advice.

Thank you to my family for putting up with my crazy obsession with fictional characters.

All glory goes to my Lord and Savior, Jesus Christ, who enables me to do all He calls me to do.

If you enjoyed *Beauty in Hiding*, would you leave me a review at your favorite retailer and, if you're so inclined, on Goodreads or BookBub?

Sign up for my newsletter to receive a free copy of Convenient Lies. You'll get information about future books, including the next book in this series. I promise not to sell or share your email with anybody, and I promise not to send you stuff every day. I will share my life with you a bit and, of course, tell you about my books and those of friends of mine that I think you'll enjoy.

Thank you for reading! Nothing makes me happier than to share my stories.

In Christ,
Robin

Connect with me:
http://robinpatchen.com

ALSO BY ROBIN PATCHEN

Beauty in Flight

Beauty in Flight

Beauty in Hiding

Beauty in Battle

Hidden Truth

Convenient Lies

Twisted Lies

Generous Lies

Innocent Lies

Other Books

Chasing Amanda

Finding Amanda

A Package Deal